Long Weekend

SM Thomas

Written by:
SM Thomas

Published by:
A.R Hurne Publishing

Edited by:
Allison Reinert, A Favorite Pen

Cover Art by:
Adrijus – Rocking Book Covers

ISBN
978-1-7396769-9-5

Dedication

For DH, AH and RH – none of this
would be possible without you.

SM Thomas

CONTENTS

Long Weekend

Chapter One

This is the one and only time we will tell Emma's story in this level of detail. Although we understand that the press and public are keen to learn about the events that took place during those four days, we hope that by presenting Emma's story in this way, we can have the space and time to process that weekend privately.

We understand that by releasing this book we will no doubt inspire further headlines but at least they will no longer be guesswork. Or, let's be honest, at times slander, to those who died during those nightmarish four days. Hopefully, this will satisfy your appetite for this case and the world will eventually lose interest in this story. I'm sure there will be one or two true crime podcasts out there that will feature Emma's story as an episode but other than that we truly hope that her name and experiences disappear into obscurity. We don't want to think of her in that way, living through that experience, any more than we have to.

To assure you we have cooperated with the police throughout their investigation, and that we take our responsibility to this case seriously, all of the text that follows in this book has been scrutinised by them. They have allowed us to publish it in the belief that it may help in the eventual arrest of the culprits of these appalling crimes. We will not publish any of the photographs taken on Emma's camera from that weekend. The police have returned the memory card to us and we're currently discussing how and when to dispose of it. There are images on there that certain families never need to see; that no living person outside of a courtroom ever needs to see. The card is being kept secure in case the police require further copies for evidence for any possible future investigations. This is the only reason we haven't shredded it yet. Once convictions have been made though, we will make sure that those photographs never see the light of day.

You are about to read Emma's first-hand account of that long weekend, written as she lived it. I'm sure some will disparage this as being the truth, but that's for them to decide. We're not here to convince anyone one way or another. We just <u>need</u> to share Emma's story. We need her words to mean something. Writing has always been therapeutic for her. Since she was old enough to hold a pen she made it a habit to keep a diary. Everyday occurrences from the mundane to the dramatic, were recorded in her handwriting for posterity. Her mother used to joke she was always working on her biography and now that gentle parental teasing has come to fruition.

We all need emotional crutches to survive, especially those who have experienced trauma. If Emma hadn't had her notebook during those four days I truly don't believe she would have remained sane. She would have been driven mad by the horror she witnessed. The terror she heard. The grief she felt.

But I'm getting ahead of myself here.

I'm sure you, dear reader, would love to skip ahead to the final chapters but please resist the urge. This story is about so much more than death. Racing ahead for the gory details might lead you to miss all the nuanced moments that happened during that time. You'll miss the memories of the people she met and their legacies. The moments of kindness and solidarity. The secrets that were unearthed.

So please, I implore you, allow Emma to guide you through this story as fate guided her through reality, and then, hopefully, when it's over we can part ways as old acquaintances. A face whose name you can't quite place. A fuzzy memory of a time long ago.

Hopefully, you'll forget all about us in a few years; I only hope we're as lucky.

Christopher Bailey
Attorney - Hanson, Cherry & Kearney Associates

Chapter Two

I can't deny the bubbles of excitement in my stomach as I'm driven to the airport in a private car. So this was how Rebecca lived. It must be nice to be the boss. Must be nicer to be the daughter of the man who owns the company but still - resentment aside, this peek behind the curtain of how the other half lives will be enjoyable.

I know Rebecca offered me this ticket as a way to placate me after turning down my request for a pay-rise last month. All it's done so far though, is show me a lifestyle that will be forever kept out of my reach if I keep being her assistant. She's never going to promote me or recommend me for a different position in the company - one with an actual career ladder, because heaven forbid, she might have to learn how to use PowerPoint herself.

True, at just over fifty thousand pounds a night, the monetary value of this holiday far outweighs the meagre five percent uplift I was asking for in my annual salary, but a once-in-a-lifetime trip is hardly something I can take to the bank and use for something useful. My fridge is on its last leg but I can hardly use photographs from one expensive vacation to replace it when it eventually dies. I guess it will be a diet of instant noodles until I can afford to get it fixed. Again.

I try hard to focus on the positive aspects of my life right now. Trying to remember all the notes from the gratitude journal Mum gave me for Christmas.

Only five other people in the entire world are going to experience the level of decadence that awaits me at the Hotel Horizen. An uber-exclusive resort, set on a small private island, featuring a gated community of six luxury apartments on a complex that boasts a swimming pool, tennis court, Michelin star restaurant, and all the beauty treatment facilities you could wish for. At least I'll be able to cling to the memory of these four days when I'm eating my fifth dinner in a row of the supermarket's finest own-brand noodles.

Nervously I pull at the shirt I'm wearing, it's not quite designer but I think it's passable. I spent all of last week scouring the charity shops nearby to try and dredge up something that wouldn't make me stand out as the outsider that I am. Rebecca had also given me a few hand-me-downs over the years we've worked together, and as I have a less-than-stellar social life, they've all lived in my wardrobe in the bags she passed them to me in. People who have money in life don't flaunt it. The clothes that they wear are of good quality but aren't flashy. That's what new money does. Some of the wealth present this weekend will be nearly as old as the salt in the sea.

What my uptight boss Rebecca doesn't know though is that as well as writing a fluff review piece for her magazine, I'm also going to write an exposé on the wasted decadence I'm about to find myself thrust into. A true glimpse behind the gilded curtain, I want to use my platform, my voice to highlight the difference between the rich and the poor. Between them and us. Hopefully, it will pay off and I'll be able to quit being her assistant. If it doesn't, I'll be unceremoniously fired so I guess I'll be living on instant noodles even without my fridge breaking. Like Dad always used to tell me though, you miss all the shots you don't take.

I've never been to a private airport before, and the lack of security presence unnerves me. There's no queue of stressed families and individuals desperately trying to reach the lounge so they can enjoy an overpriced coffee and a glossy magazine. There's no bored security guard slowly waving us all through the full body scanner or mishandling our personal possessions through the X-ray. Nobody even asks to look at my passport. It's assumed everything is legitimate and I'm welcomed on board the plane with a glass of champagne and find a cashmere blanket waiting for me in my seat. Well, I call it a seat. It's more like a double bed - far comfier than the one I have at home. I'm the first one to board and I'm enjoying the solitude when it's broken by the arrival of my fellow guests.

First to step foot on board is Fiona Appleton. Her family owns the largest money printing press in the world, if you have a note in your pocket, the chances are the Appleton's have their fingerprints all over it. Unlike a lot of inheritors of family wealth, Fiona still works at the company. If reports are to be believed, she works harder than anyone else in the business, taking the legacy of her father's family seriously every day of her life. She's a striking woman, which isn't surprising given the perks her wealth affords her. Perks that were almost taken from her thanks to her grandfather. But thankfully the racist old coot popped his clogs before he could disown Fiona's father for having a relationship outside of the 'norm.' And by the 'norm' I mean outside of the curdled eggshell their family tree was so fond of. Her parents faced a lot of hardships from both within the family and the boardroom but they rose above it all and eventually produced Fiona. It's something she discussed much more eloquently in the biography she released last year, which I may have read more than a few times.

She's forty-nine years old, married to the job, and doesn't look a day over thirty. I can tell from her hand luggage that an apothecary of creams and lotions helps her maintain her youthful complexion, as well as a subtle facelift she gets topped up every few years. The gossip forums I lurk on are always full of candid shots of her leaving a surgeon's office but they're never clear enough for any of the major magazines to publish so nothing has ever been confirmed. I'm definitely going to spend some time this weekend peeking at her face for some tell-tale scars. She smiles at me warmly and I feel bad for concentrating on her vanity rather than her achievements in life.

"Hello, I'm Fiona." She offers me her hand to shake and I take it. Her grip is firm but friendly. She isn't trying to intimidate me. "I'm Emma," I reply, waiting for her to ask me what it is I do or who I am. But she doesn't pry, instead taking the seat across from me. She places her bag beside her and turns to engage me in conversation, but before she can we're joined by another guest.

Robert Castro, of the Castro Family. A long line of famous actors and heartthrobs that have ruled over Hollywood for a century. Their names on movie posters always guarantee a smash hit and just like his father, Robert has left a trail of broken relationships behind him, both his own and others. Robert, or Bobby as he often goes by, is forty-two years old and has never dated a woman over twenty-eight. Both of his ex-wives had been twenty-five the day he'd put expensive, one-of-a-kind, rings on their fingers. Both were served divorce papers by his assistant on their twenty-seventh birthday.

I can't hide the flush that rises to my cheeks as I remember the teenage crush I had on him after his first big blockbuster- the movie that cemented him as a star. Before then, he'd mostly starred as the funny best friend in romance flicks or had brief stints in various soap episodes. I watched his entire back catalogue in the first month after falling under his spell in the cinema. My mum used to groan in good nature as I suggested yet another of the films that held his name in the credits as our weekly movie. I loved Friday nights growing up. We'd all snuggle up under one blanket on the 'big sofa' and watch a movie together. No phones, and no interruptions. Just us sharing 120 minutes together.

My dad would half-heartedly remind me I wasn't allowed to date until I was at least twenty-one, making throwaway comments about Robert Castro's suitability as a husband until I'd huff out loud and defend the new love of my life. My friends were all in the same boat. Bobby Castro was the perfect man as far as any of us were concerned. One day he'd walk past our classroom and notice one of us. We'd catch his eye and the rest would be history. It didn't matter that we lived in a pokey small seaside town that nobody had heard of and that he lived on the other side of the world in the States.

One day he would find us. We knew it. And finally, he had.

My hand longs to grab my phone and snap a photo of his profile as he takes the seat just behind Fiona. The girls in the long-discarded message chain would flip out at my proximity to him. Of course, we'd all grown up since then, most of them had found adequate husbands of their own and settled into the life they were always meant to inhabit. Plus the seemingly never-ending articles about Robert's 'love-them and leave-them' approach to life quickly ground our rose-tinted glasses to dust. He wasn't the perfect man. He was just a good-looking one. There is a stark difference between the two.

By the summer of that year I had gotten over my crush on Castro Jr. I'd moved on to the next up-and-coming heartthrob but I couldn't help the nostalgic swell of excitement growing in my stomach at the idea of spending a long weekend with him. Perhaps some of those steamy teenage fantasies I'd indulged in could finally come true? At thirty-two I was a little out of his typical age range, but so long as he didn't see my passport, I was sure I could still pass for late twenties.

I had to hold in an audible groan as the next guest boarded. I saw his name on the itinerary but had desperately hoped he wouldn't be able to make it. Lucas Jones. Twenty-eight years old and already a millionaire at least eighty times over. He started building his online persona at eight (thanks in no small part to his parents) and over the last twenty years had become the most watched person on the Internet - which is no simple task considering the sea of influencers and celebrities constantly vying for his crown. As a child he reviewed toys, as a teenager he would livestream himself playing the latest games, and now as an adult, he reviewed products for whoever offered him the most cash. Maybe I was just being cynical. Maybe his tastes were as eclectic as his social grids made out.

Despite only being four years older than Lucas, I can't help but feel like an old woman as I take in his appearance. Wireless headphones hanging precariously out of his ear, branded laptop bag slung over one shoulder, whilst the other had a tablet tucked into his armpit. His sunglasses were folded and perched on the neck of his white t-shirt and as much as I hate to admit it, the tightness of the shirt was just right - just enough to let anyone interested know that he had more than a passing interest in his home gym.

Next to board was an ex-politician who would now do anything for money, Michael Samson. If I thought Lucas's arrival signaled the barrel we were scraping, then Michael's arrival showed me just how wrong I'd been. Aged forty-six and on his second wife: an aide he just happened to fall in love with shortly after his first marriage ended. He had been forced out of politics when his peers became too ashamed of his antics and didn't want to watch his back anymore. A few leaked memos here and there and life in the House of Commons was over for poor Mr. Samson. It didn't help his cause that those leaked memos exposed quite how terribly he failed the country time and time again.

And so began the publicity campaign, because without attention or adoration from the general public, Michael would fade away into obscurity.

Something he absolutely couldn't stand for. First came the reality shows where he made cringe-worthy small talk with the other contestants as he willingly undertook any and every task that was put before him. He was a team player. He was one of us. Yada yada yada. Then came the singing contest for charity, see, he could laugh at himself too. Isn't he a good guy? And finally, he landed a regular spot as a correspondent on a popular panel show and now it felt like his murky past had never happened.

I watch as he makes a spectacle of greeting the cabin crew, repeating their names back to them to show he is committing them to memory. Finally, he turns his attention to the four of us already seated. I hear the background noise of Lucas's music grow in volume and have to bite back a smirk. It seems I wasn't the only one on board who dreaded the idea of being stuck in a luxury tin can with the man. Noticing that nobody was reaching out to shake his hand, Michael smiled to himself, shrugged his shoulders, and disappeared from my line of sight into one of the front seats. I can hear him muttering to himself about the attractiveness of one particular hostess in his plummy English accent - the kind you only obtain with a privileged upbringing - and a shudder tickles down my spine. I guess his second wife is no longer ticking all the boxes for him.

I can't help but notice the cabin crew as they check their watches regularly. Clearly, the last guest to join us is running late. They whisper between themselves and I watch with interest as they try to mask their annoyance behind professional smiles. I was all too familiar with that habit having to employ it myself many times when Rebecca would ask me for something far-fetched. Or blame me for something she'd forgotten. I try to flash a sympathetic smile towards the cabin member nearest to me and then remember that as far as she was concerned I was like every other passenger here. Full of wealth and luxury, unable to relate to their daily struggles.

"I'm so sorry!" A woman's voice calls out to them as I hear heels teetering upon the stairs. An enormous hat enters the cabin before its owner does. "I am so, so sorry." She reaches out to the crew and shakes each of their hands as she moves down the aisle toward the last vacant seat. She makes eye contact with them ensuring that they feel the sincere depths of her apologies. It was working. The crew all smiled back at her with genuine warmth in their eyes. And I wasn't surprised, she had, after all, built an entire brand based around kindness.

Her name was Penny Atwell and she was the world's most successful television host. Originally a singer on Broadway, she soon turned her attention and infectious nature towards the small screen where she won over oceans of fans with every episode and interview. She was always the person with the scoop, the one who could sensitively approach any conversation with any kind of person. Never snippy or patronising. She was, in short, perfect. And I could sit here and hate perfect Penny, but it wasn't a simple task. Unlike a lot of celebrities who paint themselves as being a good person, Penny and her wife put their money and time where their mouths were and regularly donated to worthwhile causes or volunteered for local clean-ups. Most of the time without inviting the press.

The only time she did phone the news desks was when she felt the cause she was supporting needed more awareness. If she hadn't made those calls, then people like me would never have known just how dedicated she is to making her corner of the world a better place.

Because life is vastly unfair, not only was Penny a lovely example of a human being, but she was also a gorgeous one. The laughter lines around her eyes only served to remind you of the beautiful smile she often wore. If anything, they added an air of radiance to her perfectly symmetrical face. Her black skin was well moisturised and luminous, and, today at least, it seemed that other than a quick flick of mascara and lip balm, she wasn't wearing any makeup. Because surely the universe couldn't have blessed her with those eyelashes, they have to have had a helping hand. Her hair, which she usually wore in some style of braid, was currently pulled back into a bubble ponytail that hit the very bottom of her spine as she walked. A lesser woman may try to fight Penny's naturally pleasant aura and hate her, but I wasn't a lesser woman.

Penny finally took her seat and the cabin doors closed. It's been a while since I've flown, so I'm not surprised by the ball of anxiety that's growing in size in my stomach. I take a deep breath and try to exhale my worries away. Everything is going to be fine. The life insurance cheque for each of the individuals aboard would mean the aircraft has been checked, checked, and then checked again. Nothing will be left up to chance.

Leaning back into the plush pillow behind me I

reach for the glass of champagne that's been placed on the table to the side of me and allow myself to enjoy the luxury I'm cocooned in. When in Rome, I guess.

Chapter Three

There was a touch of turbulence during take-off but nothing too severe. A couple of glasses of champagne fell over but they were replaced, generously. I look across the aisle at Fiona and return her smile as we both unbuckle ourselves.

Michael let out a comedic sigh as I heard his seat belt snap back into position. He expects somebody to respond to his overt show of relief, but so far, it was as if he had never uttered a sound. Either the other passengers hadn't heard him or they shared the same level of disdain towards him I did. Unfortunately, as the person sitting directly behind him, I had nowhere to hide. He sits up on his knees, flings his arm over his seat's headrest, and turns to look back at the rest of the cabin. I don't divert my eyes quickly enough and he locks onto me.

"Bit of a bumpy start, eh," he grins at me widely so I have nowhere to look other than at his unnaturally straight teeth. I remember when I first saw him speak at a press conference and he had crooked and slightly stained teeth, just like the rest of us. Apparently, a dental makeover was a key part of his PR strategy. Perhaps he was hoping to conquer America next. They did, after all, often make fun of Brits for the state of our smiles. I'm self-conscious now for having smiled at Fiona. My teeth weren't the worst in the world, but they certainly couldn't hold a candle to the perfect set Michael proudly held in his mouth.

"Uh-huh." I don't want to utter any words to this man. Not right now when I have no escape or viable excuse to disappear. If I engage with him, then I know I'll spend the next five hours inside this tin room with him talking my ears off. I can't allow that, but I have nothing in my carry-on luggage that I can use as an excuse to avoid him.

"So, you were saying earlier about how much you loved this book?" Fiona has turned herself towards me and is holding a paperback out across the aisle. Michael's eyes light up when he sees this as an excuse to insert himself into fresh company. "Sorry, I forgot to hand it back to you before take-off."

"Oh yes, yes I, um, read it all in a single sitting," I reply as I take the book from her with a grateful nod of my head. Turning the book over in my hand, I see that it's the punchy thriller everyone has been talking about online. I'd kept meaning to pick up a copy but never got around to it. And to be honest, when I had the choice between spending £9.99 on a book or a bottle of wine to spend my evenings with, the same company always won out.

"Is that the book that all the 'celebs are talking about?" Michael puts air quotes around the word celeb and my insides cringe on his behalf. "I've never been a big reader," he proclaims as though it's a badge of honor.

"You don't say," Fiona delivers witheringly before pulling her eye mask down and reclining in her chair. I couldn't contain the giggle that escapes my lips and I momentarily experience a pang of guilt as I notice embarrassment flit across Michael's face.

He clears his throat, clearly trying to shake off the cutting words from Fiona's tongue, and turns his attention back to me. By now though, I've already cracked the spine of the gifted paperback and am making a show of being drawn into its first chapter. He watches me for a minute, waiting to see if I will be polite and acknowledge him, but thankfully I'm more protective of my mental health than that. Five hours of conversation with this dreg of society would not put me in the best head space to enjoy my weekend. As much as I'd spend this weekend building up titbits for my article on wealth disparity, I also wanted to indulge in some much-needed rest & relaxation.

It's what Rebecca wanted after all - a way for me to return to work with my head back in the game. She seemed to think it was stress that was causing me to be a little less dedicated to her life than usual. In reality, I was bored. I'd outgrown my role and knew she had no intention of letting me strengthen my roots and grow. Plus, it doesn't help that my wage stagnates as much as I do. I'm meant to do more than this with my life. I know I am. I just don't know exactly what that hypothetical 'more' is yet. I thought I'd have it figured out by the time I hit thirty, but two years later, I'm still clueless. Then again, there are a lot of things I'd assumed I'd achieve by my third decade on the planet. Just like most other people, I guess.

Fiona is feigning falling into a deep sleep to avoid any further awkward conversation. I wondered if she'd known what she wanted to do with her life all along and then quickly scolded myself for being so foolish. She'd probably never had the chance for a career wobble given she inherited her family's printing company at a relatively young age. To have a career wobble would risk destroying her family's legacy and foothold in the world - neither of which she would risk.

I'd read an essay she'd penned once about being a so-called 'nepo baby.' Unlike others, she didn't shy away from the fact she was born into a world of privilege that most of us would never achieve. She was aware of her luck in the great lottery of birth and wasn't shy about owning up to it. It made her a much more endearing character, making her wealth easier to swallow. Those she worked with always spoke so highly of her and her work ethic that it wasn't hard to believe that in some small way, perhaps she deserved everything she'd been born into. At least she wasn't blind to her good fortune, unlike some other billionaires.

As though my thoughts had summoned him, Robert Castro appeared in the aisle between us. He clears his throat and I can't help but allow my attention to be drawn to him. Years of teenage obsession simmering to the surface. I guess no matter how the years age someone, there's always something comfortable about slipping into the past.

"I don't believe I've had the pleasure," is his opening line as he extends his hand to me. My stomach turns to jelly and I was grateful once again for the paperback that Fiona had lent me. It meant I had something to do with my hands. Suddenly, I'd forgotten how to use my arms. Looking towards his outstretched hands I remember how many times I'd imagined his fingertips on my skin on those sweaty teenage nights. Christ, I'd had my first sex dream about this man and now he was standing in front of me, so close I could smell his aftershave. Woody and old-fashioned - I wasn't surprised.

"Emma." I finally stutter out in response before

moving my hand towards his to shake, forgetting it still held a paperback novel enclosed. He laughs in a way that makes my heart sing. It was the laugh I'd played over and over in the interviews he gave around his blockbuster breakout movie. My dad had teased me relentlessly by learning to mimic it and pulling out his new party trick on every occasion. No. I definitely don't want to be thinking about my dad right now. Nausea momentarily replaces lust in my stomach, but I shake it off as I put the novel down and finally take his hand.

"And my name's Robert, but everyone calls me Bobby."

"Which do you prefer?" I'm taken aback by my confidence. What on earth has come over me? I can't seriously believe that Robert Castro, of all people, actually wants to engage in conversation with me. He probably wants to ask to borrow something or whether I knew our estimated time of arrival. He certainly hadn't approached me to connect. I could feel the warm heat of blush painting my cheeks and settling on the tip of my nose.

He considers my question for a moment, kindly indulging me in conversation when, obviously, he wished to be anywhere else. I was thirty-two now, for Christ's sake, no longer a giggly teenage virgin. I should be able to control myself better than this.

"He prefers Robert," interjects Fiona, her eye mask still pulled down as a sly smile now creeps across her face. She has a beautiful smile.

It was obvious that there was some kind of history between the two of them. I make a mental note to only address him as Robert from now on. Then curse myself a little for being so cringe-worthy that I believe that what I call him matters. He'll have forgotten my name by the time we land. Why should he remember it when someone like Fiona has a level of familiarity with him?

She was phenomenal, not just in her work ethic but in her looks as well. When she'd first arrived on the plane, I'd noticed she was attractive for her age, but now up close, I could see that she would pass as attractive for my age. Hell, she'd be attractive for any age.

Her skin was blemish-free, unlike mine, which was littered with freckles and a post-PMS breakout. I honestly thought that turning twenty would mean the end of acne, but every month on cue, my chin erupted into a hormonal minefield.

Fiona's hair was well-kept. Each strand seemed blissfully hydrated and arranged poetically. Whereas mine was dyed using a colour mask every three days. I couldn't afford a trip to the hairdresser regularly, so had to make do with a quick and easy online solution whenever my pay cheque allowed.

Robert cast his eyes over Fiona and seemed confused as to why she was wearing an eye mask when suddenly the reason appeared before him. Michael turned himself backward in his chair so he could face us and join in on our conversation. I resented him for bursting this bubble of privilege I was on the cusp of infiltrating.

Michael summons a crew member over with a flick of his wrist, barely glancing over his shoulder. As the flight attendant reaches his side, he turns to look at her, his eyes scanning her body leisurely. Reaching out his hand, he places it in the small of her back, which forces her to lean down towards him. The backs of every woman on board tighten in unison. We've all been in the same position at some point, touched by a man who isn't welcome.

"Could I have a rum please, beautiful?" he asks. The flight attendant smiles at him awkwardly, straightens her back, and makes a show of taking a step away from him. His hand hangs loosely in the air and he flexes his fingers as though he is merely stretching. I watch as she makes her way down the aisle, back towards her colleagues, all of whom have looks of concern written on their features.

"It is an absolute pleasure to meet you, Bobby," purrs Michael, turning his attention back to the surrounding celebrities. Robert considers him for a moment.

"You're the politician, aren't you?"

It felt like more of an accusation than a question, but Michael shows no signs of feeling flustered.

"In a past life, for my sins." His throat attempts a self-deprecating laugh, the noise it emits however is closer to a quack.

"Nice to meet you." Robert offers him his hand and the two men shake for slightly longer than they should. I can tell that Robert was leaning into years of PR training to play nice but I wondered if Michael was too. The tension in their wrists as they shook hands was obvious to me. I just wasn't sure why.

"Looking forward to this weekend?" asks Michael.

"More than you realise. I've come straight from a press junket and am really looking forward to four days away from the world." He chuckled as he finished speaking but I could tell from his shoulders that he was stressed. I hadn't been aware that he had a new film coming out. It shows how much I've outgrown my crush on him. At thirteen there wasn't a single television appearance, much less a new film of his, that I would miss. I had three photos of him on my wall after all. Once again I felt my face flush at the idea of Robert blatantly knowing just how attracted to him I'd once been. Borderline obsessive, as most teenage crushes were.

"What are we all chatting about?" her voice is so familiar to me that I don't find her arrival jarring. It's as though I'm sat at home with the television on, her show in the background to my mindless doom scrolling. Penny is now standing at Robert's back, stealing glances at Fiona as she tries to squeeze herself into our little group. Could perfect Penny perhaps have a little crush on Ms. Appleton? A trickle of jealousy creeps down my spine, which I try to dismiss. Fiona is nobody to me. I am here for one reason - to write a story about the disparity between them and us and to kick-start my career as a journalist.

Even so, Fiona and I had briefly bonded over our avoidance of Michael and I didn't like the way Penny looked at her. Especially when Penny was essentially the spokesperson for having a happy marriage. With her wife in mind, my eyes flick down to her hand and I notice with interest that she isn't wearing her wedding ring. Trouble in paradise?

Seeing that Fiona hasn't acknowledged her presence, she turns her gaze towards me and not so subtly looks at the space on either side of me on my giant seat. I try to hold in a sigh, which I know is unkind, as I shuffle over and make space for her. I'd much rather share my seat with Robert, or Fiona, but I guess Penny would have to do, and at least it was another person to keep Michael entertained.

"Thank you so much. My name's Penny." She doesn't offer me her hand to shake. Instead, she flashes me her very best talk show host smile. I can't help but return it, despite my jealousy over her potential interest in Fiona. I can't deny the kindness that emanates from her. No wonder her guests always feel comfortable enough to share their secrets, warts and all. I feel like I could tell this woman anything and she wouldn't once judge me.

"Emma, would you like another glass of champagne?" Robert cuts me off before I can respond to Penny's introduction and I notice the cabin member standing in front of our group.

I nod at Robert, conscious not to move my head too much, lest I look like one of those nodding dogs my mum insists on keeping on her car's dashboard. He hands me a glass, leaning over Penny as he does so, and if I didn't know any better, I swear she bristles at his presence.

"Perhaps we could have a couple of bottles to keep on hand?" Fiona speaks, pushing her eye mask off her face and sliding up in her seat to make space for Robert. He gratefully takes the seat next to her and I watch to see if I can catch the secret touches of lovers between them. There is definitely history there. But it doesn't happen. Their body language is relaxed and devoid of any sexual tension. Perhaps I misjudged their connection. Men and women can just be friends.

The crew member nods at her request and as she moves away from us, Fiona reaches into her purse and pulls out two fifty-pound notes. "Let's make sure we tip generously." She shoots a look at Michael in particular, who becomes tongue-tied and turns back to face the front of the plane.

It's only then that I notice the absence of one of our party. Lucas is still sitting by himself at the back of the plane, the tinny sound of his music only growing in volume as the five of us socialise. Part of me wants to mention this oddity to Penny, sure she would want him to join us. She's a Good Samaritan like that and wouldn't want to leave anyone out.

I lean my head closer to her and just as I'm about to mention Lucas's absence in a stage whisper, Fiona calls my name across the aisle and suddenly I'm engaged in a conversation about who I'd screw, marry or kill out of the latest cast of an action blockbuster. It feels strange to be playing this game with people who could be friends with the subjects, but I don't want to seem like a killjoy, so I give my answers. They amuse Robert, who throws his head back with a hearty chuckle. Leaning forward in my seat I catch Fiona's eye who raises her glass in agreement with my choices.

I almost want to ask Penny to swap seats. My neck will become crooked from the constant leaning around her to engage with the others. She doesn't want to converse with Robert or Michael, but I know that would look too obvious, and it would cause offence.

She's leafing through the paperback Fiona lent me, and I have to fight the urge not to slap her hands away as she cracks the spine further. I'd been hoping to keep my memento from this flight in near pristine condition, but by the time we land, it will be dog-eared; its pages covered in grease from her fingers.

Once again I spot her missing wedding ring and

sympathy takes over my feelings towards her. I wonder what has happened in her marriage. It always seemed so solid on the outside. They always put on a united front. Then again, that's the problem, isn't it? These are the types of people who only show you what they want you to see.

Taking in the guests around me, I'm sure that this weekend will be full of experiences most people would kill for. I'm going to be sure to enjoy as many moments as possible, without forgetting my main aim, of course.

Before I boarded the flight, I hadn't been sure whether to anonymise the names in my story, but having met the people I'll be writing about, I have decided that I will. Possibly because I now see them as human, but it's more likely a desperate bit of hope that after this weekend we might stay in touch. A girl can dream.

Chapter Four

As the plane touches down, my head is swimming with champagne. The giggles that won't stop spilling from my lips are an octave higher than usual. I pull my hand away from my hair untangling my fingers finding I've twisted three strands of it into a knot. Why do I always insist on playing with my hair when I'm nervous or drunk?

Fiona peeks across at me from behind Robert's back and wiggles her empty glass to see if I want a refill. I make the sensible decision for the first time in five hours and shake my head in response. She pouts comically at me and I'm almost swayed to change my mind, if only to impress her, but then she puts her empty glass on the table in front of her and claps her hands together.

"Right, I think we've all had enough to drink!" There's an audible groan from Robert, Penny, and even Michael who managed to insert himself into the fun eventually, as the alcohol caused memories of his interaction with the flight attendant to take on a blurry haze. They all put their drinks down one by one.

"Ladies and Gentlemen, we're preparing for descent. Please return to your seats and fasten your seatbelts." For a moment nobody moves in response to the cabin crew's directive and then, all at once, Penny and Robert stand, causing them to come to a halt facing each other in the aisle. Suddenly the carefree atmosphere we'd all cultivated comes to a halt.

"Ladies first" offers Robert after a beat, taking a step backwards to allow Penny past. She doesn't acknowledge that he's spoken and walks in front of him back to her seat. Robert, fueled by the half a bottle of whisky he's indulged in, pulls a face to her cold shoulder. But he doesn't call her out on her rudeness. He still has some level of self-control. I can't believe what I've just witnessed. Penny Atwell, the queen of kindness, has a mean streak like the rest of us. I just wish I knew what Robert had done to offend her so greatly.

The silence that has now descended across the plane is peaceful. I hear the melodic click of five seat belts being brought together before I follow suit. Here's where the weekend really begins.

We're due to land at the airport nearest Hotel Horizen. Because it's based on a private island, we'll have to ride there on speedboats. I am not the world's biggest fan of the sea but thankfully the liquid courage I've just indulged has me feeling a little braver than I was this morning.

When Rebecca had given me the itinerary for the weekend and I saw boat travel was essential, I nearly turned down her offer to take her place. She scoffed at my nerves and explained that travelling on a speedboat was nothing like travelling on a booze cruise. She assumed that had been my only experience of sea travel, and, to be fair, she wasn't wrong, but it had still stung to hear her pin me so basic.

We land without any issues, for which I am grateful. Michael makes a show of loudly applauding the pilot for a job well done. I cast a glance in Fiona's direction and she raises an eyebrow in response. Out of everybody on this trip, I can't believe it's bloody Fiona Appleton that I've bonded with the most. She's a feminist icon whereas, some days, I still wish for somebody to ride in and change my life for the better.

To tell you the truth, in the five hours I've spent in her company, I can safely say that I have developed, for want of a better word, a girl crush on her. But as is always the case with my sexuality, I'm not sure if I want to be her or be with her. Either way, it didn't matter because either option was an impossible pipe dream.

With smiles that must have taken hours to perfect, the cabin crew stood in the aisle, opened the plane door, and ushered us down the stairs. I notice Robert slipping a piece of paper to the youngest-looking one and have to resist rolling my eyes. He really needed to stop being such a cliché if he wanted his career to continue thriving. The older he got, the wider the age gaps, and the bigger the creep factor. We're told our luggage will be transferred to the boats for us and there's nothing for us to do other than head to the harbour and enjoy the sunshine whilst we wait to board.

Feeling the heat beat down on my skin, I'm glad I snuck into the toilets an hour ago to apply my Factor Fifty. I burnt like a peach even on a cloudy British day, let alone in the tropical heat that awaits us at Hotel Horizen. There's a man with a little white captain's hat perched precariously upon his head, waving at us from the harbour. Robert and Michael stride ahead from the group to greet him. I'm walking in pace with Fiona and Penny and wonder to myself if anybody watching would believe that I could fit into this group - just another millionaire out for a weekend break.

Glancing behind my shoulder, I notice Lucas has finally removed his headphones but he's dragging his feet so he doesn't have to walk with the rest of us. Perhaps the internet's number one socialite isn't that social after all. Emboldened by the champagne, I smile back at him, and surprisingly, he returns my gesture. I'd expected him to either blank me or roll his eyes given he's spent the entire flight avoiding interacting with the rest of us. As we reach the harbour, I notice Robert looking rather annoyed as he ends a conversation with the Captain.

"Two per speedboat," Michael exclaims with a dorky smile on his face. Perhaps I ought to be a little kinder to him. He's the only person here who's actively showing his excitement about this weekend. Maybe he's more self-aware of his good luck than the others. Then I remember his hand in the small of the flight attendant's back. The lies he told in Parliament. The awkward reality show appearances where he pretended to be 'one of the people.' No. I shouldn't be any kinder to Michael than was necessary.

"The boats are already assigned," said Robert, and now I understood his tight jawline. It was a little patronising that we weren't trusted to pick our travel companion. I was about to speak up in agreement with Robert when I noticed little signs appear at the back of each waiting speedboat. I'd been assigned to share the journey with Fiona. My irritation with feeling patronised soon evaporated as I sent a little thank you up to the heavens for my good fortune.

"It's only an hour, Robert," chastised Fiona as she began walking towards our boat. I looked at the remaining boats - Robert was travelling with Penny and Michael with Lucas. Robert looked relieved, probably to see he hadn't grabbed the short straw and been subjected to one-on-one time with Michael. At least the two social outcasts were assigned to each other.

Penny looked as though she was about to murder somebody. She was quickly turning into the most interesting character on this trip - so very different from what I assumed she'd be. I watch as she takes a step towards the Captain and he shakes his head. She stalks away from him towards the waiting speedboat and Robert follows sheepishly behind. Just what happened between the two of them that's caused this much animosity? And why does it seem so one-sided?

Lucas is standing with his mouth open in shock as he shakes his head and takes a step backwards. Michael, on the other hand, is already making himself comfortable on board. My parents raised me to be a polite individual and I curse them for it at this moment.

"Everything okay?" I ask.

"I'm not going with him." Lucas's voice is deeper than I remembered. Perhaps he raises it a couple of octaves when creating his content to appeal to a younger audience? Whatever the reason, his proper voice suits his face more.

"It's only for an hour." I try to reason with him, hoping this will be the end of the conversation, as I can see Fiona waving at me from the deck of our boat. There's a rumble through the air as the engine of Penny and Robert's boat starts up, and then they are gone, skating across the ocean toward our destination.

"Swap with me?" he asks.

This man, who has barely even acknowledged my presence in the time we've all spent together, actually dares to ask me for a favour.

"No swaps allowed. Insurance purposes state that you need to be in your assigned boats. In case of accidents." interjects the Captain who is now standing in front of us. My stomach drops at the mention of the word accident and I try not to think about the vast ocean between the port and our final destination.

"Madam, if you could please join your companion, we are ready to depart."

I nod at the Captain and look at Lucas once again. I can see the flicker of fury ignite in his eyes. Surely he can't be this upset over being saddled with Michael? He needs to grow up a little, as we'll all be spending the next four days within orbit of each other. Unless he plans on spending all his time in his room just to avoid awkward conversations.

"Just put your headphones in," I suggest as the Captain holds out his arm to usher me to the boat.

Lucas blinks, gains control of his anger, and nods his head. Fishing his headphones from his pocket, he walks towards Michael and their waiting boat.

"What on Earth was that about?" asks Fiona as I am helped onboard. She's desperate for gossip, and I'm happy to indulge her. As I fill her in on Lucas's discomfort with Michael, she moves in closer towards me, our thighs touching with her face inches from mine. She tells me it's because of the roar of the engine. It's the only way she can hear me properly, but the heat between us tells me otherwise.

"Don't let them drag you into their drama," she says as she places a hand on my leg. "This weekend is about you. Having fun. Remember that." There's a glint in her eye as she speaks and I'm drawn towards her lips that are raised in one corner, as though she's holding in a smile. For a moment, I wonder if she's about to close the space between us and place her lips on mine. Sadly, the boat's Captain shouts something towards us and breaks the moment.

Chapter Five

The hour-long journey passes by in a flash, as we chat nonstop about topics that in all honesty don't have any real bones to them. It feels comfortable to talk to her. Words are easy to find.

Before I know it, the island appears on the horizon. As we drive towards the small jetty, the sight of it takes my breath away. It's an absolute slice of heaven hidden in the dreamy blue ocean. Even from this distance I can make out the sandy white beaches framed by luscious greenery, I really am the luckiest girl in the world right now. I pull out my phone, hoping to send my mother a quick snap of the paradise that stands before me, but find that my signal is lacking. Still, that isn't enough to dampen my spirits as I take in the golden sand and lush woodland that awaits me.

The hotel was located a short walk toward the centre of the island, and as we are guided there, I drop away from the group a little wanting to take in every inch of this new and fascinating world around me. Nobody else seems that taken with the scenery we were walking through. I guess they were all used to seemingly untouched private islands, but not me. I was in awe of every palm tree and flower I walked past. Even though I had no signal, I took as many photos as I could before the guide shot me a scolding look. Clearly, I wasn't behaving in the manner that was expected from one of their posh guests. Feeling reprimanded, I slip my phone back into my pocket.

To avoid summoning another one of the guide's disapproving glares, I drop away from the group even further, choosing to take a side path – whilst following the others on the main path. I don't want to get lost, not completely anyway. Just lost enough to explore the surrounding island. Large Hibiscus plants pop up everywhere, in an entire rainbow of colours.

In between them are plants I didn't know the name of, but I take photographs so my mother can identify them when I get home. A large purple flower that appears to have tendrils growing amongst its petals catches my eye as it weaves itself amongst the surrounding foliage. If I were someone who could realistically afford to be here this weekend, then I would be sure to have that flower growing in my garden every season. A large red insect flies angrily into my face. It buzzes around my ear as I try to remain still and not panic. This is enough to drive me back to the main path and the rest of the guests. I've never been the biggest fan of things that fly. Especially ones that cannot be identified.

The stairs leading up to the hotel were coated in blue and white mosaic. It must have taken somebody hours to painstakingly place each piece individually. I could picture them sitting out here, basking under the sun, lovingly crafting the steps that my fellow travellers were traipsing up with no regard for the beauty that existed below their feet. This was just another staircase to them, just another path to a weekend of luxuries. I can already feel my fingers itching to work on the exposé. To highlight perhaps, how a life of money can blind you to the beauty in the world it gives you access to. Robert turns around to smile at me as I make my way up the last few stairs.

Perhaps my article could wait for a few more hours.

He held out his hand in a gesture of chivalry, to help me up the last step, and his palm lingered on mine for a moment longer than necessary. Yes, I definitely have time for at least a drink before I retire to my room and start writing.

The six of us stand in front of two large white doors. Penny is looking around them for a doorbell of some sort. In the distance, I can hear the symphony of the speedboats' engines as they start up and cruise away. It's silly, I know, but it leaves me with a sense of unease. Like we've been abandoned. On either side of the doors are large mirrors and watching our reflection through now sober eyes, I understand how out of place I look. Despite having drunk more than me, each of my companions still looks put together. As though they've just walked off a magazine shoot. Whereas I already have a sheen of sweat on my forehead and chin and my hair more knotted than when we left the plane. Maybe having a drink right now wasn't the best idea. I should go to my room and freshen up.

"Surely they know we've arrived?" asks Michael. He turns to look at the guides who brought us to the bottom of the staircase. But they've vanished. None of us noticed them leave and they didn't bid us farewell as they did so. Not the best customer service.

"Perhaps they're preparing the welcoming party," reassures Fiona. She could be right, it would make sense that they'd want our arrival to cause as much fanfare as possible. This is the calm before the luxury storm I'm sure.

Penny turns to look at the rest of us, avoiding Roberts's eye line as she does so. There's a look of concern on her face and I imagine mine is mirroring hers. I can feel the soft cold fingers of anxiety beginning to weave themselves around my throat. What if we aren't expected to arrive today?

What if somewhere in the organisational chain, a date was mistyped, and there are no staff on the island today to let us in? My eyes dart around us as I take in possible shelter options. Could we break in? No. Surely, between the six of us, we could survive one day roughing it in the surrounding nature. I doubt there were any dangerous animals for us to worry about. An up-market establishment like Hotel Horizen wouldn't want to risk the deaths of their guests via the jaws of something scary.

Just as I'm about to suggest we find somewhere to shelter and make a plan of action, the doorknob begins to turn. Two attractive male attendants pull the doors wide open and lock them into place, grinning at us widely. I feel mildly embarrassed at my lack of funds as I watch Robert shake their hands - slipping some currency into each. I have a tiny stash of notes hidden in my suitcase, saved up over a matter of weeks to tip any staff I'd encounter this weekend, and it undoubtedly won't be enough.

We walk through an archway and then we're inside the main resort area. From this spot, I can see at least three swimming pools with picture-perfect blue water, two tennis courts, what looks like an outdoor spa, and a restaurant. I was sure there'd be more to discover over the next four days, but even from here, this place blew my expectations out of the water.

Around each pool are daybeds that look like king-size beds, with fabric draped over the top of them to provide a little shelter from the sun. On the side of each bed, I can see a table jutting from the frame and I'm already fantasising about relaxing on one whilst reading the paperback Fiona lent me, a glass of something sweet waiting for me within arm's reach. The cushions, placed perfectly on the bed, looked ready to swallow me whole. Especially after our long journey. I was ready to sink into their Tiffany blue embrace. Once I've cleaned myself up, I'm going to make a beeline to one of them. Maybe I'll invite one of my new friends to join me. Then when the sun gets to be too much, we could take a dip in the pool, and make use of the swim-up bar before relaxing in the comforting haven of the daybed. This weekend was certainly going to be more enjoyable than I'd originally expected.

"Welcome to Hotel Horizen." A gentleman in a starch-ironed white shirt and black trousers approaches us with his arms outstretched. He speaks in a language I don't recognise to the two male attendants who pick up our luggage and close the doors behind us.

"My name is Stephen, and I will be your main point of contact for the weekend. You have any problems, they become Stephen's problems." He mused at his sense of humour and I join in because the crowd surrounding him has grown chilly in the atmosphere.

The bubble of excitement we'd created for ourselves on the plane popped when we were forced into assigned seating on the boat journey. Still, I wasn't about to let an hour of annoyance ruin three nights and four days of what was shaping up to be a utopia. A female attendant in a grey polo shirt displaying the Hotel's logo arrives at his side and he guides us to the centre of the resort.

"Your luggage is being delivered to your suites as we speak. My colleague Sam here will check each of you in. If you could provide her with your passport so she can check the details over at the Guest Services desk, that would be appreciated."

He nods his head towards a small information centre, tucked away to the side of the restaurant, and Sam makes her way towards it. Michael is the first to step forward, passport in hand and smile on face. I am bouncing back to thinking I've misjudged him. He seems to be the only other person here who isn't sulking about the last hour of our journey. Well, other than Fiona. But since departing the speed boat and approaching the hotel, she kept her distance, which surprised me given her behaviour on the boat. I must have misread her signals - imagined there was a spark between us when she was just being polite. Why would somebody like that be interested in someone like me?

I'm tapping my feet absentmindedly when Stephen approaches me with a barely concealed expression of annoyance on his face. It's a stark contrast to the customer service smile he'd flung at me moments before, and I wish that one of my fellow guests would appear at my side so they could witness it too. There's something in his eyes that makes me feel uneasy, a level of frustration that I don't have a name for. On instinct, I take a step back from him, putting some distance between us.

"You're not on the guest list." His tone is dripping with accusation and now the reason for his anger is clear to me. Rebecca didn't let the hotel know of the guest's name change. She didn't ask me to swap it and I, in my stupidity, just assumed that for once she'd taken care of the finer details given this was supposed to be a treat for me.

"Didn't anybody call ahead?" I know the answer but I'm stalling for time, not sure what to do. If he throws me out of the complex and sends me home, I'll be humiliated. I won't have the chance to conduct my research and write my article. I can't let that happen.

"You aren't Rebecca Marsh." It is quite clear from looking at me that I'm not Rebecca Marsh. She's a beautiful five-five Black woman with the world at her feet. And I'm five-nine in flats with a complexion the colour of cow's milk. We were polar opposites.

"Unfortunately, Ms. Marsh had a last-minute appointment come in." I instantly revert to my assistant voice - the one that's been honed thanks to years of mind-numbing customer service jobs. The tone is polite and carries an edge of empathy within it. The perfect way to apologise to or for your boss without actually admitting you or they've done anything wrong.

"She kindly offered me her ticket."

"The tickets were non-transferable." His words drip with disdain. How was I supposed to know that this trip was meant for Rebecca and Rebecca alone?

I barely had the chance to glance at the invite when it landed on my desk before she whipped it away in excitement. Everyone who was anyone had applied to attend Hotel Horizen's opening weekend and she'd been ecstatic to have made the final cut. My only involvement after that was to call up and make the payments. Everything else had been organised by the hotel itself - I hadn't even needed to book her flights.

She'd actually said to me that I was lucky to not have to worry about sorting out this trip for her. What she didn't understand was that having someone else controlling her diary set my teeth on edge. There was no way the hotel would know her preferences, and somehow, I'd be the one who took the blame when it all went tits up. She was predictably unreasonable like that.

"Oh." I don't have any excuses lined up for this issue, as I wasn't aware of its existence. Trust Rebecca not to read the small print. It was a miracle I'd been allowed to board the plane, all things considered.

"There weren't any issues with my flight though."

"That was organised by a third party who should know better than to allow unexpected," he pauses on that word in particular, letting his tongue roll over it, "guests to board." That would explain why my name had been on the sign on the boat. They would have created them based on our boarding information. I should have known better than to assume it had been because Rebecca had taken care of things.

I could feel tears prickling at the corners of my eyes. I was embarrassed and frustrated. It wouldn't be long before someone noticed this conversation and found out I was a fraud. It was a miracle nobody had asked who I was yet, especially when everyone else on this trip was a household name. Maybe they'd just assumed I was a broker who made a lucky trade or something.

I'd already dreamt up my backstory and practised it so many times it felt real.

I would explain my ability to afford this trip because of a recent lottery win. I'd opted not to go public with it because of the problems that money can cause. I'd pause at that point to allow them an empathetic statement. They'd know first-hand how money can colour the relationships around them. Then I'd carry on and explain that I'd put my name forward for this trip as a late-night moment of euphoria after finding out I'd hit the winning numbers, never expecting to be picked.

They'd be charmed by my commoner tale and intrigued by my plans for my newly found fortune. It would be the perfect cover for the weekend and now Stephen, this man before me, was threatening to pull it all apart before it had even begun.

His face softens as he takes in my expression and he places his hand on my arm. When he wasn't scowling, he had the kind of smile that made you want to open up and spill your heart out to him. He glances at either side of us before leaning in closer.

"I won't tell anyone if you won't. Just be careful this weekend. These are not your people." He nods his head at me and turns to walk over to the check-in desk where his colleague Sam is waiting to serve me. I hadn't noticed because of my interaction with Stephen but each of the other guests is walking in differing directions towards what I assume is their accommodation for the weekend.

I guess none of them noticed the fact I'd been pulled aside by the concierge for a private chat. Or if they noticed, then they didn't care enough to intervene, even when I'd become distressed. No. They couldn't have noticed. I'm sure even the socially distant Lucas would have come to check to see if I was okay if he had.

"This is Emma Jones, a special guest who had the good fortune to join us this weekend." Stephen is introducing me to Sam, and I nervously smile at her. I'm not sure what exactly made him warm to me suddenly but I was grateful for it.

"Sam here will make sure you're checked into one of our very best suites."

Briefly, she shoots him a questioning look. Probably wondering why he isn't sending the usurper back to the airport. I know that on her screen the last guest she is expecting is Rebecca Marsh, not the mysterious and maybe important Emma Jones.

"Are you sure?"

She doesn't hide her displeasure at my existence, and I don't blame her. I won't be a big tipper this weekend, not that I don't want to be, but I'm unable to be, so why should she bother to pander to me?

"Yes." Stephen fixes her with a look, telling her to remember her place and she cowers beneath it.

"Of course." This time she turns on her best smile and shoots it at me. "I'll have your room information ready for you in a moment." She bends down and rummages through a little drawer behind her desk.

"Have a wonderful stay with us, Emma." Stephen smiles at me as he makes to leave.

"And remember, be careful this weekend."

Finally feeling welcome at Hotel Horizen, I relax and look around my surroundings, taking in the opulence. Then something hits me, a small trail of cold creeping its way up my spine. I never told Stephen my name.

Chapter Six

I vaguely follow the direction in which Sam pointed. There had to be an explanation for this. Stephen must have been given my details by the travel company.

"Wait!" Sam calls out after me, emerging from behind the sanctuary of her desk. I turn to look at her, finally feeling my pulse calm now that I've figured out how Stephen knew my name. The crew that brought us across had to have updated him. Or maybe he saw it on my luggage tag. A sane, perfectly legitimate reason for him knowing who I was.

"Yes?" I stop walking and wait for her to reach my side. She holds out her hand expectantly and after a beat, I offer her mine to shake. It seemed unusual, but I didn't usually run in these kinds of circles, so had no choice other than to follow her lead.

"Your phone?" she requests, removing her hand from mine to hold it out, raising an eyebrow in amusement at my faux pas.

"Huh?" I can't help the noise that comes from my mouth in response to her question. I know it makes me seem dim but I don't have a clue what she's talking about.

"All guests must check their phones and any devices capable of taking images. These will be held by the desk for the duration of your stay. You'd have known that had you received the welcome packet in the mail."

A thinly veiled reminder I'm not supposed to be here, and one that instantly makes me nervous. Was I really expected to hand my phone over to this woman for the next four days? What if there was an emergency? What if I woke up with perfect hair and had to take a selfie? What would happen to my game streak in Candy Cruiser? Like most people my age, it felt like my whole life was contained in that little electronic rectangle and I wasn't keen on handing it over.

"Can't I sign a waiver or something promising not to take photos of the other guests?"

A snort of derision escapes from her nose. Samantha certainly isn't a fan of mine and isn't afraid to let it be known now that Stephen was out of earshot. All I can do is hope that she has a quick change of heart towards me, just as Stephen had. Soon she'd mellow and realise I was somebody just like her - somebody who counted every penny that came in and out of their account, and struggled to make ends meet as payday approached.

"A promise can always lead to temptation. This way there's no chance of any accidents happening."

"What if there's an emergency? I haven't even told my mum I've arrived safely." I pull my phone out of my pocket and click the home button. My background image is a hastily snapped photo of the family dog, taken when she first joined us ten years ago. Bella was an old woman now in terms of dog years, but I never tired of looking at the tiny sprite of a thing she used to be. There's no signal or 5G symbols on my screen. I have no chance of using my phone as anything other than a camera for the next few days anyway.

"We have a landline behind the desk in case of emergencies." She's still holding out her hand expectantly and I hand my phone over to her.

"Do you have any other devices? Tablets? Laptops?"

I nearly laugh at the idea of using my laptop as a camera. It's so bulky and as with most laptops, the camera quality is shocking. Rebecca refused to upgrade it for me. Even during the pandemic, when every meeting was conducted online, I had to exist in blurred-out low pixels, like something from the earlier noughties. It hadn't even crossed my mind to bring it with me. I always preferred writing in my notebook anyway.

Despite knowing that I have a relic of a digital camera packed in my suitcase, I shake my head. I need some images of the hotel to accompany my story about this weekend, and hopefully, I'd have a balcony where I could take them privately. I hadn't intended to pack it until my mum pointed out that my phone battery might die, and she would hate to miss out on any snapshots from this holiday.

Satisfied she has now robbed me of any recording devices, Sam walks back towards her desk with no further conversation. She may only be doing her job, but that exchange had felt a little personal. I pull the handle of my suitcase up and continue walking in my appointed direction.

My accommodation appeared to be in a different direction than everyone else's. I could see Fiona retreating in the distance. Just as I wonder if Sam had sent me on a wild goose chase, a small building came into view before me. It wasn't as ostentatious as the ones I'd walked past on my way down this path, the ones that were probably holding my fellow guests, but to be honest, that suited me. This entire island was a little intimidating so it was nice to be on the outskirts, a poetic representation of my social status.

I walk through a small archway. I could tell from the wet patches in places that the bricks were freshly washed. At least this means they'd always intended to use this room in some capacity. They hadn't just sent me here as punishment for being a stowaway. The sounds of my feet climbing the stairs echo around the empty corridor. The door is pulled too, but not quite shut. They must have left it like this when they dropped off my luggage. On closer inspection though, something about this door is different. There's no keyhole, no scanner for a pass, and no form of technological thumbprint-operated lock. Walking into the room, I turn and close the door behind me. There was a door chain on the inside frame, but still no lock. What was I expected to do when I left my room?

With a slight shake in my hand, I put the chain in place and then take a deep breath. There would be a reasonable explanation for this. Besides, it's hardly like I had to worry about anybody breaking in and stealing my belongings. For a start, all the other guests here could buy and sell what I'd brought with me a thousand times over, and then there was the case of how a thief would abscond with my belongings. Hotel Horizen boasted on its website about having the most secure leisure facility in the world. Therefore, even if somebody with bad intentions wanted to steal my bargain basement pyjamas, they wouldn't be able to get off the island without alerting us to their presence. No. Even without a door lock, I was quite safe here. I was still grateful to have the chain though.

Now I'd comforted my nerves, I finally turn

around to survey what would be my temporary home for the next three nights. My hand instinctively reaches into my pocket for my phone to document this, but it comes back empty. Instead, I had to make do with taking a mental picture and notes to refer to at a later date.

In front of me was a corridor with a rug so plush laid out across it that my feet sank into its depths. I followed the rug, kicking off my shoes as I did so, into the main room and nearly gasp at the sight before me. Huge floor-to-ceiling windows framed the wall before me and through them, I could see two comfortable chairs, oak decking, and a small pool laid into the floor. I could walk from my bed straight into it if I wished.

Before I moved onto the balcony though, I looked at the bed. It was easily bigger than the king-sized one I ordered for Rebecca's new home. I wondered if I'd feel lost sleeping within its many inches of space. My bed at home was barely a double. It left just enough space in my bedroom for a small bedside table, but I wasn't willing to purchase a single bed. They were for children was the argument I made to my dad as he helped me carry the mattress up the stairs when I first moved in. He'd grumbled about his back but still insisted on carrying my last box of belongings into my new flat. He was a gent like that.

On either side of the bed were large rectangular tables, easily the size of a small chest of drawers. The mahogany of them gleamed, and I wondered how hard they were for the staff to keep clean, certain that the grease from my fingertips would leave behind marks if I even dared to brush against them. To the right of the bed was a chaise longue complete with enough pillows to suffocate a large man, and to the side of that was a standalone claw foot bath. Moving towards the bath to get a better look at the other side of my room, I noticed a handrail and some steps leading down into, yes, leading down into a hot tub. I could happily live in this room for the rest of my life. It has every luxury I daydream about and then some.

If this were the accommodation for usurpers, then I couldn't fathom what the other guest rooms would look like. My suitcase is lying neatly at the bottom of my bed and I'm relieved to see it hasn't been unpacked.

Mum warned me that sometimes fancy places unpack your belongings for you and I didn't fancy the idea of a stranger rifling through my supermarket-purchased underwear. Plus, there was the small matter of the contraband camera I'd not declared on check-in.

Unzipping the case, I root around inside until my hand finds it. I absolutely have to take some photos of this room. Nobody back home will believe me otherwise.

Making sure the flash is off, I capture a few images of the room, the balcony, and of the fixtures and fittings around me. The sink in the bathroom had a faucet shaped like a golden swan. Mum would find that most amusing. Ducks were more her thing, but I knew she'd appreciate that even rich people enjoyed decorating with birds. I can almost hear her exclaiming to Dad that she was inserting a bit of luxury into their lives the next time she came home from the garden centre with another ceramic duck.

I'm struck with a little homesickness as I think about my parents. I hadn't lived with them for a few years, but I made a point of talking to them both at least once a day. Even if it was nothing more than a funny picture shared in our group chat, and now I was cut off from them and the rest of the world. If I didn't play my cards right, then this weekend could end up being very lonely indeed.

There was a melodic ringing sound in my room, and following its tones, I came across a small intercom on the wall by the internal hot tub. There's only one button nearby so I press it and hesitantly talk.

"Uh, hello?"

"Miss Jones? A welcome dinner will be served in the restaurant in an hour. We trust you will join your fellow guests?"

The voice was tinny but female. Perhaps it was Sam. Maybe she'd finally heeded Stephen's warning about treating me well this weekend.

"Oh, of course. Yes. It would be a pleasure." Be a pleasure? I sounded like such a twat.

"Marvellous. We'll see you in an hour."

The voice cuts out and my room is silent once again. Looking towards my suitcase, a sense of worry settles in my stomach. I should have asked what the dress code was for this meal. I don't have many high-end outfits with me and didn't want to waste one if everyone was staying casual for dinner. The clock in the room's corner seems to grow louder and more ominous with its ticks whilst I stand motionless in the middle of my room, paralysed by the fear of doing the wrong thing.

"Nobody dies, Emma." I tell myself. Somebody in my talking therapy two years ago once explained that this was the phrase they used to keep themselves grounded when panic arose. It made sense at the time and I've used it several times since then. Especially when Rebecca heaped stress on my plate which was already overflowing.

"Nobody dies." I repeat.

Chapter Seven

As I pull on the hem of my thrifted dress, worrying about whether I'm about to make an utter tit of myself, I long for my phone. That way, I could quickly look up how many people have actually died of embarrassment in history.

I'm sure it must have happened at least once or twice, and I certainly didn't want to be the first. If I were the first reported case of death by embarrassment, they might name the phenomenon after me, and that would be enough shame to haunt me in the afterlife.

Now I know that this moment in time was nowhere near as important as a surgeon removing a brain tumour, but it would shape the next few days and decide whether my career after this trip as a journalist would truly begin. If it all went wrong, if I didn't make the right impression and became the social outcast of the group, then I'd be stuck following Rebecca until the end of my days.

The dress I'd chosen was a simple cotton cream strappy number that brushed just above my knee. I'd sat and considered Fiona and Penny's outfits from our journey out here and had concluded that only new money, such as Michael's or Lucas's, shows its hand. Fiona had worn an over-large shirt and a pair of tight light jeans, and Penny had been wearing a simple black and white maxi dress. Neither of them had designer luggage or accessories, so I'd kept my outfit as simple as possible to blend in.

As I walk up the path towards the restaurant, I know I've made the right choice. Fiona raises a well-manicured hand to wave me over to a table on the veranda. They've found a spot that granted them shade from the sun that was still beating down and my complexion was grateful. I reapplied my sun cream after my shower but hadn't brought it out with me as I wanted to travel light.

It had made me nervous leaving my room door unlocked. I guess I just had to trust in the resort security, as I'm sure every other guest had. Besides, if someone broke into my room they'd quickly move on to another after finding my belongings. The only thing I bothered to hide was my notebook and camera, which I stuffed in between some folded towels in the wardrobe. I didn't want those items slipping into the wrong hands.

Robert pulls out a chair for me as I approach the table, a spot between him and Fiona. I couldn't have been happier with the seating arrangements. I thank him and sit down as gracefully as possible, trying not to scrape the chair on the floor as I pull it in underneath me. Penny and Lucas sit opposite me and Michael has taken one head of the table's position to Fiona's side. Everyone seems relatively at ease in each other's company, unlike the way they'd seemed on arrival, and I smile appreciatively as Lucas reaches across the table to fill up my wine glass. Before the conversation can begin, Stephen arrives at the table.

"Today's meal is a tasting menu. The chef has prepared dishes local to us to give you a sensory journey through the island. I trust you will all be pleased with your food, but if anything is to your distaste, please let me know and we can arrange some more regular options if so desired." I'm sure I'm being paranoid but his eyes rest on me as he thinly describes someone at the table as potentially having a lesser palate than their dining partners. The joke's on him though, I've yet to meet a meal I haven't enjoyed.

With his declaration, he leaves the table with a flourish and we descend into a comfortable silence. Determined not to be the one to break it, I take a sip from my glass and look at the resort around me. Whereas before I'd been too rushed and stressed to take in the full splendour on offer, now I had the time to commit it to memory, ready to write about later. The sand around the base of the veranda was so white it looked as though it had been spray painted. A gentle breeze encourages it to dance amongst itself, causing a rustle as it blows up against the well-maintained greenery.

Directly in front of the veranda is an ashy jetty that runs into the large lake of seawater that takes centre stage in this part of the island. It must have taken some serious manpower to fill and I follow the trace of it until it disappears behind the high walls that keep us safe from prying eyes.

On the jetty are two woven sun beds, and I give thought to asking Fiona if she fancies meeting there after breakfast tomorrow morning. Or maybe I'll see if Robert would like to start the day with a quick swim. My head is giddy thanks to the wine and the lust coursing through my veins. It was all hypothetical though. They didn't have that kind of interest in me. In fact, following their exchange on the plane, I wondered if they had an interest in each other.

With this thought in mind, I didn't miss the conspiratorial glance between the two of them right before our first courses arrived. It was certainly charged but I couldn't pin down what was behind it. The smell of our starter course filled my nose and distracted my brain. Some kind of seafood. Penny was apprehensively poking it around her plate with a fork. I catch her eye and take a quick bite of mine.

"Fish and garlic." I simplify the tastes that are whirling down my throat into the two largest flavours for her. She smiles at me before taking a bite. I hadn't had Penny down as a fussy eater. Surely she attends many events with her wife where she doesn't get to decide what she eats. I would have thought she was used to a culinary surprise by now.

I repeat the exercise each time a new plate arrives. Penny pauses and waits for my comment. I disguise it as an outward exclamation of pleasure each time, not wanting to draw attention to the fact I was helping her decide which dishes she could stomach and which she could not. When a dish wasn't to her taste, she'd explain to Stephen how her palate needed a little cleanse before sipping the lemon water he supplied her with. It was the perfect play, and I couldn't help but notice Stephen's disappointment each time he came back to clear our plates and found mine just as empty as the others. I thought he'd changed his impression of me upon check-in but it seemed he still viewed me as the other, the lesser than. I was just grateful that so far he hadn't outed me.

"So, Emma." Michael had made sure there was a

pause in the conversation before he spoke. "I know of all the other guests this weekend, but you appear to be a mystery."

There it was. The suggestion of a question I've been dreading and anticipating in equal measures. What Michael meant to ask was, who are you? What have you done to earn your place here? Why do you deserve this as much as us? I'd hoped to at least get through this meal without having to rely on my acting skills, but it seemed I wasn't to be that lucky.

"Well, it's a rather boring story really," I begin, putting down my knife and fork for effect. I saw Stephen out of the corner of my eye pause in the doorway with our next course. He didn't want to interrupt my performance and the sly smile at the edge of his lips told me he was looking forward to the show.

"I won the lottery two years ago. Not a life-changing amount but a solid nest egg. Thanks to some smart investments on my broker's part, I haven't had to work since." I hope this is the end of the interrogation, and I'm relieved to see Robert, Penny and Fiona all nodding their heads at my completely plausible explanation.

"How clever of you." Michael's tone was anything but congratulatory. "How strange, though, that we've never heard of you."

"I kept the win a secret. Money can change relationships." Something I've heard Rebecca say countless times when she had been betrayed by another confidant.

"You must give me the name of your broker. I keep meaning to make some investments myself." Why won't Michael drop the subject? Have I made some kind of mistake that's pegged me on his radar?

"Simon Fishter." The name of an ex-boyfriend. One who had been a rising star in the personal investment field. One whose star client when we were together had been Lucas Jones. Thankfully, I'd never attended any of the functions Simon's company had put on to entertain their clients. I'd been too busy working on my own professional path, believing back then that the late nights at Rebecca's side would eventually lead to a real career in journalism.

"Great guy," interjects Lucas, and I smile at him gratefully.

A good lie always has an ounce of truth, and Simon had been a great investment banker, even all those years ago. His clients loved and respected him. At Christmas, we were practically drowning in thank-you gifts from them. He used to try to sell at least 50% of the material gifts he was sent - the watches and clothes, using the money for his own investments and to pay down the mortgage on his flat. He was very sensible, that Simon.

One of the main reasons we broke up was because of how dull I found his stability back then. With hindsight though, he was probably the best of all my partners. Perhaps if I'd stuck with predictable Simon right now, then I wouldn't be stressing about the cost of the supermarket ramen versus the name brand.

"Simon, Fishter," repeats Michael, as though he was jotting it down in his mind. "Perhaps you could give me some pointers this weekend?"

"I'm afraid I don't have any idea where my money's kept. Simon keeps all the details from me. Otherwise, he knows I'd be obsessively checking the market every hour."

"Oh I'm the same," interjects Fiona with a laugh and I smile at her gratefully. "I never know what shares I'm invested in until I get the dividend statement at the end of the quarter." I'd taken a gamble on that part of my story. I hadn't prepared and researched a lie in advance, so I was relieved to hear that Fiona felt the same as I'd implied. It meant I was still on the right track.

"Anyway, Michael, it's so gauche to discuss finances over dinner, don't you agree?" now it's Robert's turn to come to my defence. Michael's cheeks flush a light pink and he nods his head.

"Of course, of course. Sorry, everyone. I'm just new to this," he gestures at the complex around us, "style of living. I was hoping to pick Emma's brain to try to make the most of my money whilst I have it."

"My advice, Michael?" Penny has now turned to him and I can't read her expression. Her lips are tight but her eyes are soft. "Live like this as little as possible and you should be fine."

Michael nods and she turns her attention back to her plate. We've just been served a salad and she's confidently picking her way through the leaves without my guidance. "I wish somebody would have told me that." She adds to herself between mouthfuls. If anyone else has noticed her aside, they make no show of it. As we all finish the salads in front of us, Stephen steps out of the restaurant empty-handed.

"Oh, thank God!" cries Fiona jokingly. "I'm fit to burst!"

"Ms. Appleton, would you like to have a break before we move on to the next course?"

"I think that might be a good idea Stephen, thank you." She's become, at least for tonight, the unofficial spokesperson for us all.

As Stephen retreats into the building, the rest of the guests and I let out happy groans. Robert makes a joke about undoing his belt buckle and I blush as I find my eyes drawn to his crotch. He notices and flashes me a wink before turning his attention back to the group. Or at least I think he winked at me. Maybe there was just sand in his eye.

Fiona places her hand on my upper thigh as she laughs at a story Penny is explaining.

"Oh, you must hear this, Emma," she exclaims, her hand remaining on my skin. My dress that had once sat just below my knee was now raised on one side, Fiona's side, and it allowed me to feel the heat from her palm. I was sitting between two of the most attractive people on earth and they were both paying me a level of attention that I hadn't even received from people I had seriously dated. Was it possible that both Fiona and Robert had me in their sights, just as I had them in mine?

My head is spinning again thanks to the alcohol, sexual tension, and laughter around me, and I stand up from my chair. Robert and Fiona both move to stand alongside me, asking if I'm okay and I wave them away.

"I'm fine, honestly. I just need to stretch my legs. Walk off some of that food before they bring out the next course." It takes some convincing but I manage to get both of them back into their seats so I can enjoy some time alone. I need to clear my head. My fantasies were running away with my logic and I couldn't let that happen. I had to stay focused this weekend. I had a story to write.

I walk down the jetty next to the veranda and sit on the edge of it. Untying my sandals, I let my feet drop into the water. It's cooler than the sand I've just walked across but not cold. The sensation is instantly soothing, and I wonder if I could get away with spending the rest of the night out here. My throat's dry though, eventually, I'm going to have to go back even if it were only to grab something to quench my thirst.

As though summoned by my thoughts, a bottle of water appears at my side, along with a shy cough.

"Mind if I join you?" asks Lucas as he pulls off his loafers and sits down next to me. I'm not sure what to make of the fact that he made himself comfortable before I had the chance to reply.

"Of course not."

"You seem to be making quite the impression back there." He smiles at me and I busy myself unscrewing the water bottle. Maybe I didn't imagine the attraction between Robert, Fiona, and myself. If Lucas had picked up on the atmosphere between the three of us then it must have been there.

"Am I?" I don't want to seem cocky, I need to play it cool. As though famous millionaires are always falling for me.

"I don't know what you've done to land on Michael's radar, but I feel for you."

Oh. So he wasn't speaking about Robert or Fiona. I guess I may have blown their behaviour out of proportion ever so slightly. Got carried away with the fantasy of a holiday romance. There was a lot of resentment in his tone when he spoke Michael's name.

"You don't like him much, do you?"

"I thought I'd been so subtle." He laughed at himself, knowing full well he's been wearing his heart on his sleeve ever since he lay eyes on the man. "I know the truth, by the way."

"Which one?" I'm trying to keep my voice level and nonchalant.

"I know who you really are, Emma. I'm guessing you didn't know Simon kept a photo of you on his desk?"

He's right. I hadn't known that. By the time we broke up, we'd only been together for nine months. I hadn't realised that was serious enough to warrant a spot on his desk. Two years later and Lucas still recognised me from a snapshot on his broker's desk - what were the chances?

"I'm very good with faces. Names, not so much, but I never forget a face." He smiled at me. "I'm not going to tell anyone, just so you know. I don't have a clue how you found yourself here but you have to remember to be careful. These people aren't who you think they are."

Chapter Eight

"What do you mean?" I ask. I'm intrigued by the seriousness knitted between his eyebrows. Could Lucas know something that would make for a juicy side story in my exposé?

"Exactly what I said. No one here is what they seem."

"Everybody has secrets, Lucas, even you, I'm sure."

He looks uncomfortable, and I know that I've hit a nerve. I don't know why I'm so defensive of my fellow holiday-makers, but I can feel my jaw growing tense in frustration at his insinuation.

"Like you say. Everybody has secrets. But all secrets aren't created equal." he says, speaking with an eloquence I hadn't expected from him. Too used to viewing him through the lens of social media. I almost expected him to shout out that this exchange was a prank as his catchphrase was pumped across speakers around us, a setup from his earlier days of streaming. But no big revelation came. Or at least not the kind I was expecting.

"Michael took bribes that resulted in the fire at that care home." He doesn't need to say which care home. We'd all watched the news footage in horror as the flames leapt up the floors two at a time. The shock on my face must have been noticeable because he pressed on.

"He let them bypass building regulations, health and safety procedures, and capacity guidance. He knew he was going to leave politics eventually and wanted to make sure his pockets were generously lined before then."

The fire in the care home had been front-page news for weeks. Thirty-six residents had perished alongside ten caregivers in a matter of hours. Those who survived the initial blaze were still being treated for physical and mental scars.

It had shocked and gripped the nation. Thankfully, the fire brigade had contained the flames to the care home itself and prevented it from spreading to neighbouring businesses and residential homes. But the saving of some lives didn't take away from the tragedy of losing others. The judge on the case had ruled it the fault of the night manager and the poor man's reputation had been forever tarnished.

His family had spoken out in his defence to try to get the public to see that one man shouldn't be held responsible for so many failings. Failings that were outside of his pay grade and decision level, but nobody cared to listen. He'd perished in the fire too, unable to even defend himself. His grave forced to be moved to an undisclosed location to prevent people from vandalising his resting place.

"My nan died in that home," he said.

So there it was. The actual driving force behind Lucas's distaste for Michael. It wasn't just about Michael's shady values and dodgy dealings, as slimy as they were. It was personal.

"I'm writing an exposé on him. Well, not just on him. I've got a whole series planned." He glances over his shoulder back at the veranda, but I can't tell who in particular he has his sights set on. A shiver runs down my spine as my imagination flits toward the darker side of life. Wondering what secrets my other travelling companions may be hiding that were as 'interesting' as Michael's.

Lucas is no saint though. If he were, he'd hand any evidence he had over to the police and let them deal with it. Instead, he'll use his platform to expose them and gain a steady stream of revenue. I imagine the irony of his grand plan is lost on him. And if he succeeds, he'll cement himself for another year as the internet's most popular streamer. People love a morbid story. I myself am partial to the odd murder podcast. If it bleeds, it leads.

That's the phrase my journalism professor had tried to drill into us. The more tragic the story, the better the ratings. And he wasn't wrong. The facts were there in black and white. Newspapers containing images of the Twin Towers falling had broken historical sales records. Podcasts about true crime were always higher in the charts than those about less sensational topics. We all enjoy the macabre side of life far more than we care to admit. Christine, one of my fellow students, had been incandescent at this phrasing though. She'd told him as much.

In all honesty, that was the moment I'd fallen for her. Something about the fire in her belly and the passion from her tongue was intoxicating. Her anger at the world had grown tiresome eventually though. Deep down, I was like most other people, happy to settle for a peaceful life. And that's when Simon entered the picture.

"You could help me, Emma. I've seen the way they've all bonded with you. You have access to them I'd never be able to secure on my own," Lucas pleaded, bringing me back to reality.

I shake my head instantly. I won't even entertain this notion. I had my own article to focus on, a far less flamboyant one. One that wouldn't blow apart the lives of those around me. I just wanted to highlight the wealth, and therefore, lifestyle divide between them and us. I didn't want to destroy them.

"That's not going to happen."

"Will you at least keep an eye out for anything suspicious? I meant it when I said you need to be careful. Those people over there are capable of things you couldn't imagine. You need to watch your back." He doesn't wait for a response, standing up and heading back to the veranda. I watch as he waves at Penny, and I realise that Lucas is perhaps as dangerous as anyone else here. What kind of person can harbour such hatred and resentment, yet smile at the supposed perpetrators?

In the distance, I can hear Robert calling my name. I peer over my shoulder, and he's gesturing to me that the courses have started to arrive again. I guess I have no choice but to rejoin the party. I don't know for sure that what Lucas has told me is true. I have no doubt that he lost someone in the fire itself. Many people did. But to lay the blame solely at Michael's feet without sharing solid evidence with me made me distrust him slightly. Grief can warp a person's logic. We always need someone or something to blame for the loss of a loved one. To accept that some things are a random act is unpalatable. Every action has a cause.

The question I had to ask myself, however, was, could one man, even one as untrustworthy as

Michael, really be held accountable for such a catastrophic turn of events?

Heading back towards the table I try to shake my worries about Lucas. After all, I was hardly Michael's biggest fan. Politically speaking we were complete opposites, and now it turned out that we were more morally distant from each other than I'd first suspected. I knew his time in office had been filled with selfish decisions that had led to problems for people like me. You know, normal people. He had voted to cut benefits for those who needed them, was against basic human rights for those seeking refuge, and had even been absent on the day the ballot was cast on same-sex marriage. Not to mention the affair he unabashedly had whilst in office. But did I think he was so callous, so money-minded, that he would throw away so many lives just to bolster his bank balance?

I watch him chat to his fellow millionaires as I approach the table and a feeling creeps up to my throat from my gut. Yes. Yes, I believe he's capable of that. He turns to smile at me as I sit back down and I return the expression. I wasn't much better than Lucas. Smiling at the enemy for an easy life.

The rest of the meal passes in carefree conversation. I join in where necessary but spend most of my time observing the people around me with a new suspicious eye. The way Robert carved his steak with gusto, eyes briefly taking in the sharp edges of his knife for longer than was natural. Or how Fiona's hand kept finding excuses to touch my skin without invitation (granted this observation I didn't mind too much). Lucas's false laughter at any joke uttered. Michael's look of longing at Robert's designer watch. Penny's quiet and down-turned gaze. How many secrets were hidden at this table, and did I want to turn down the chance to unearth them?

Two people here had now warned me to be careful. Though Stephen's warning, at least at the time, had seemed more barbed and aimed at my behaviour than safety. With their words in mind, I now chose to keep my drinking to a minimum, despite the creeping early hangover it was beginning to invite, but it was a small price to pay to keep my wits about me. This weekend would not be as relaxing as I'd first hoped.

By the time Stephen clears away the very last of the plates, Michael is wishing us all a good night. With one hand on his stomach, it's obvious he's overindulged just as much as the rest of us. At least he has the good sense to take himself off to bed as soon as it's polite.

As for the rest of us, a day of travelling mixed with full bellies and goblets of wine led to less than sensible decision-making. Fiona and Penny grab a bottle of wine each from the table and disappear from the veranda in a fit of giggles. I watch as they stumble arm in arm towards the pool, my heart in my throat as they take a step too close to the edge. I push my chair back and stand in a panic, ready to run and jump in should one of them fall, but thankfully, they collapse laughing onto a nearby lounging set.

Robert eyes me with a sly smile. He'd noticed the way I'd worried about the two women.

"Strong swimmer, are you Emma?" he asks with a good-natured chuckle and I feel my cheeks grow red once again with his attention. I'd been so distracted by my proximity to Fiona during dinner that I'd forgotten all about the man of my teenage dreams sitting at the same table as me. I sit back down again and rest my head on my hands in a way that I hope is flattering, mostly to stop the world from spinning ever so slightly. I should have stuck to my guns and refused to drink anymore after my chat with Lucas, but Fiona had made sure my glass was topped up regularly. Penny had made a small comment about me not being able to keep up with the others and with that set off my immature and competitive nature, attempting to match them all glass for glass.

"I think I'm going to retire, too," says Lucas, standing from his chair and nodding at the two of us. I watch as he walks away down the path toward what I assume is his villa. Desperately, I wanted to confide in Robert about what Lucas had told me. To tell him about Michael's supposed crimes and get his opinion on how I should handle the snake within our midst. But then I'd have to explain how Lucas knows me. I'd have to risk him exposing me as an interloper too. And the butterflies in my stomach at Robert's undivided attention weren't worth losing.

"So, it's just the two of us," purrs Robert, leaning in closer towards me. He smells of whisky and aftershave. It's a heady mix and I want to bask in it. "The last two standing," he added with a smile.

"Robert!" calls Fiona from the lounger, as though she could sense the sexual tension brewing on the veranda. "Robert, Emma, come join us!" Her voice is light and melodic, charming beyond drunk explanation.

With a smirk, Robert stands and offers me his hand. I don't need his help to get out of my chair but

I'm not about to turn down the chance to touch his palm. It's slightly rougher than I'd imagined. I'd always thought every inch of him would be well moisturised and maintained. It was nice to realise he was, even ever so slightly, less than perfect.

"I guess we'd better join the rabble." he says.

I'm ashamed to say that I'm disappointed when he lets go of my hand after helping me to my feet. A large part of me had hoped we'd walk towards the others hand in hand, that he'd claim me in some way as his own. Then I imagined the look on Fiona's face if she'd witnessed that and a wave of guilt washes over me - how ridiculous. Neither Fiona nor Robert are my partner, and as I had to keep reminding myself, neither of them were interested in me. They were just very confident, flirtatious people. Personalities born out of a life in the spotlight. Nothing more than that.

As we approach the pool, Penny looks over and scowls in our direction. She says something to Fiona that I can't make out and moves away from the seating area. I watch as she walks to the other side of the pool, kicking off her shoes and sitting with her feet in the cool water.

"What's her problem?" asks Robert as we sit down with Fiona. She shrugs her shoulders, but as she takes a sip from her glass, I catch the glance she shot Robert. A glance that told him that he should know exactly what Penny's issue is. Then, quick as a flash, the warm smile is back on her face as she holds out a glass of champagne towards me.

"To new friends," she announces, holding her glass in the air. Robert follows suit, as do I. We clink our glasses together and agree with the sentiment. I feel a pang of guilt as I glance across the pool at Penny. The three of us have created a clique and she wasn't involved. I knew how that felt. I had often sat across the field on my own watching the 'popular' kids play out their daily dramas. A world just out of my reach.

Not anymore, though. Now I was one of them. One of the chosen ones. Even if only for a few days.

Chapter Nine

The smell of cigarette smoke tickles a drunk part of my brain I'd thought was long forgotten. It's been five years since I last had one, but right now the craving was as though I quit yesterday. Glancing over the pool towards Penny, I watch as she takes a long drag before leaning back on her hands and exhaling deeply.

"Maybe I'll go take Penny a refill." I say as I fill an empty glass. With a bit of a stumble in my step, I make my way around the pool towards her, the smell of nicotine guiding my tipsy movements. Thankfully, I managed not to spill a drop of champagne and offer her a flute with a smile.

"Cigarette?" she offers the packet to me. She can sense the real reason for my visit, but I'm not even the slightest bit ashamed of being so transparent. I nod my head and she pulls one from the packet, places it between her lips, and lights it before handing it to me. Sexy didn't come close to describing the moment and Penny wasn't oblivious to her movements. I'd never considered her a sexual person. She was like the nation's big sister. She always resisted the offers for lingerie photo shoots. Her brand was too precious to risk for a five hundred grand payment. Yet here she was, oozing sexual temptation.

I take the cigarette with thanks and sit down, taking the chance to dip my feet in the pool alongside her. Despite the magnetism radiating from Penny, I had zero interest in pursuing what it could mean. She wasn't my type. I'd tried dating 'nice' with Simon and that hadn't ended well. Unfortunately, there were very few ways in which it could have ended worse.

Besides, I had enough tension with Robert and Fiona to get me through the weekend, so I didn't need to add another potential suitor to the mix. As we sit and smoke in comfortable silence, I notice Penny is still missing her wedding ring. There's a white band on her finger where it used to lie and I can't help but stare. Alcohol robs me of any subtlety.

"It's in my room." Penny explains, having noticed the attention on her hand. "I wanted to see how it felt." She rubbed her hand absentmindedly, staring into her palm as though she were trying to read her future.

"Oh, of course." I say, acting as though I understand where she's coming from. In reality, I'm clueless about the ins and outs of a marriage. My parents had always rubbed along together nicely enough, and I hoped one day to find someone I could do the same with. Besides, perfect Penny had the perfect marriage. Why would she want to see how it felt to be out of it?

"Are you married, Emma?" she looks down at my hand, having already guessed the answer before asking the question.

"No. I don't have a partner." I let out a small laugh, wanting her to know that this doesn't bother me. That I am honestly happy on my own. Sure, it would be nice to have a little more fun a bit more often, but there are always hook up apps when the mood strikes. And the idea of sharing my life day in and day out with the same person feels rather overwhelming after my back-to-back relationships with Simon and Christine. I'm not ready to settle down again, not until I've got my career sorted, at least.

Penny smiles wistfully in my general direction, but it's clear she isn't really in our conversation. She's one foot down memory lane and I'm nothing more than someone to bounce alongside.

"I've noticed you and Robert seem close," she surprises me as she snaps back to reality. "You need to watch yourself there. He's not a good man. Not a good man at all." She throws her cigarette butt into the swimming pool and I have to stop myself from scolding her. Just because you were a guest somewhere didn't give you the authority to act however you wished. It was a bit of a dick move, but she clearly had something bigger on her mind.

"Why do you say that?" I ask. She's made her dislike of Robert painfully clear so far today and I'd love to know why she carried such disdain towards him. Just as she's about to share her reasons with me, a deep cough interrupts us.

Robert stands behind us both, hands on his hips as he eyes the floating cigarette in the pristine blue water. Penny has the good grace to appear momentarily embarrassed by her actions before she realises who's joined us. With a wobble, she stands up, aggressively pushing Robert's hand away when he tries to steady her.

"I don't need help from you of all people." Her voice no longer has a tipsy edge to it. Instead, it sounds certain, as though her hatred for him has instantly sobered her up.

"Penny, I think we need to clear the air between us."

"Oh, you'd like that, wouldn't you? Like to use your words to dig yourself out of the mess YOU made." Her voice is rising in volume as her passion grows. I'm starting to worry I'm going to have to break up a fight. The thought of this causes my happy drunken bubble to deflate. I'd never been the best at conflict. At least outside of my dating life.

"Let's all calm down." Fiona has joined us now. The ruckus draws her attention away from the bottles of champagne. "Maybe you should go and lie down Penny?" She touches the other woman's arm tenderly, a way to let her know she isn't taking sides. "Perhaps we could all meet up and chat in the morning?"

Penny composes herself, nods at Fiona, and leaves without another word. I notice she's left her cigarettes and lighter behind and I pick them up. Placing them into my pocket, I tell myself I will give them back to her tomorrow, but I already know the pack will be emptier by then. The lighter has a 'P' encrusted on it in jewels. Like the kind you find in the markets on holiday, although I very much doubt this one was haggled from a vendor in Magaluf.

"It's getting chilly," says Fiona, wrapping her arms around herself despite the balmy temperature we still find ourselves in. The sun may have set but it was easily still in the high twenties. "I have some blankets in my room if you'd like to hang out?" she directs the question at me but Robert goes to answer.

"Why Fiona, I thought you'd never -"

"Girls night, Robert. I'm sure you understand."

He shoots her a smouldering smile in an attempt to sway her but she doesn't melt under the weight of it as I would have. She's firm in her decision, and her invitation has set my nerves, and imagination, on edge. My skin is already tingling at the idea of being in such private proximity to her. I have to keep a hold of myself. She's just being friendly.

Then I remember her hand brushing my thigh and I wonder if perhaps I'm not being so unrealistic with the idea that she might be attracted to me.

"Well, I'm going to stay and finish my drink. Emma, you're welcome to join me if you don't fancy an early night."

Robert Castro has asked me on a date. Well. Not a date exactly. But he asked me to stay and have a drink. All alone. With him. It's definitely date-adjacent at least.

My heart's thumping as I look between the two of them. This can't be happening. This isn't real. Two of the most attractive people I've ever met can't be competing for my company. The plane must have crashed on the way here and this is nothing more than a prolonged coma dream.

Fiona is gorgeous. Absolutely gorgeous. With deep brown skin that practically hums with health. Her eyes sparkle as she watches me wrestle with this decision and her plump lips are drawn into a smile. She leans back on her hands as she sits beside me with her legs dangling in the pool and stretches her back, pulling it into an arch that accentuates her perfect cleavage. She knows exactly what she's doing.

And Robert. He's Robert bloody Castro. I've slept with him in my dreams more times than I care to admit. And tonight, if I played my cards right, I might get to experience his lips on my flesh. I grow warm at the thought. Would reality live up to my fantasies if I stayed behind to have a drink with him? When I think of what my decision could lead to, it suddenly becomes a very easy one to make.

"A cosy night in sounds lovely." I reply, placing my hand on Fiona's.

My friends will never let me live down the opportunity I've wasted, but this woman is phenomenal. Even if she does only have friendship in mind, I'd be a fool to make any other choice.

Robert holds his hands up in friendly defeat and walks back towards the table full of forgotten drinks. I watch as he contemplates pouring himself a fresh flute of the remaining champagne but decides against it, sending a half-hearted wave goodnight in our direction as he stumbles off down one of the paths.

The two of us are sitting in comfortable silence, our feet occasionally grazing the other's as we roll them around in the cooling water. At a loss for anything else to do, I pull out Penny's cigarette packet and light myself one. Fiona leans over, pulls it from between my lips, and takes a drag. She tries to hold the smoke in her mouth but ends up spluttering. Handing the cigarette back to me, she looks sheepish.

"I figured that would look cooler than it did."

"Not a big smoker then?" I ask.

"Honestly? I can't stand the taste."

In an instant, I put the cigarette out in the sand beside me and lay the packet and lighter on the floor out of reach. Not that I was expecting her to make a move or anything. I just didn't want to taste like an ashtray if she did.

By now we've been sitting alone together for a good twenty minutes and the alcohol in my blood is pulling me towards sleep. Fiona stands and offers me her hand.

"You coming?" she asks with a suggestive smile.

I can't find the words to respond, so I merely nod and place my hand in hers. Our fingers intertwine as we make our way towards her villa. We pass the back of the restaurant as the lights get turned out. I guess Stephen and the rest of the staff have finally closed up for the night.

I feel a prickle of nerves when I consider the possibility of him spotting me in Fiona's company. He'd warned me to be careful; warned me to keep myself to myself. And now he was seconds away from catching me walking hand in hand with the most prominent guest on the island. What would he do if he caught me in this compromising position? Would he reveal who I was to Fiona? Would she care?

It's all too much for me and my feet slow to a halt. Fiona turns to look at me, face full of concern.

"It's okay," she says. "We can just get to know each other." She gives my hand a reassuring squeeze, figuring my nerves in this moment are because of the pleasures awaiting me in her room.

"It's not that," I start. Keeping my ears focused on the noises around us, in case I heard footsteps up the gravel path. "I just. You just," I'm stumbling over my words. Is it morally right for me to go to bed with someone who doesn't know me? I don't mean like a one-night stand you pick up somewhere. That situation I'm all too familiar with. I mean, is it right for me to go ahead with this when I've spent hours in this woman's company living a lie? I am here, after all, to write a piece about her and others like her. About how the wealthy don't appreciate what they have. About how they throw their money and privilege around without a second thought for those without. Could this be construed as entrapment?

"You just don't know me." I finally stutter out the words that will be my downfall. I have to tell her the truth. I don't want this to be a one-and-done thing. I like Fiona. I already like her more than I should, and if I want her to like me back, I have to treat her with respect.

I hold both of her hands in mine and look up at her. The light from Lucas's porch shines through her thick black hair. It might be the copious amounts of alcohol talking, or the heat, but she looks like an angel.

"Then let me get to know you," she offers suggestively, leaning her body towards me. Before I can say anything else, her lips hover dangerously close to mine. Millimetres away. I can feel her breath in my chest, and all I want her to do is close the distance between us.

She doesn't, though. Not yet. We continue to stand so close that the heat from our skin merges into one as her hands find their way to my hips. Before I can stop myself, I'm wrapping one of my arms around her waist, pulling her closer to me, so close I swear I could feel the heartbeat in her chest. God, what a chest. I push my lips towards hers, an animalistic need taking me over but she turns her face slightly and I brush against her cheek. She smells like champagne and vanilla, and I can't get enough.

She turns her face back towards mine, and one of her hands snakes its way up my spine, causing a full-body shiver as she does so. She slips the fingers of the other hand under the strap of my dress, playing with it lightly, teasing me. I want her to rip it off. I need her to.

Now her hand is at the back of my neck, gripping it tightly as she finally, finally closes the gap between us, and her lips find mine. We're so hungry for each other that this is no chaste first kiss. There's passion and perhaps a touch of fury behind it. She guides my head into positions she enjoys and gives my hair a tug when I try to lead.

"Good girl," she whispers to me as we finally pull apart. I'm stunned by what has just happened. I've never been kissed like that, wanted like that. I have the sudden urge to pick her up and run back to her villa, knowing that what will happen this evening will blow my mind. I look into her eyes and I know that everything about this moment seems right.

Well. Everything except the shadow I can see over her shoulder. The shadow in Lucas's living room. The one hanging from the ceiling. Swaying.

It's not until Stephen has run to our side that I realise I'm screaming.

Chapter Ten

"You need to calm down Emma." Fiona rubs circles into the small of my back as I openly sob. "Come on now, you can't sink into this." I watch as Stephen tries the double doors at the front of Lucas's living room.

"They're locked." He presses his face up against the glass. "The key is in the lock. My master won't work."

"We have to get in there. Now." Fiona's voice is steady and firm. She's taking charge of the situation and that suits me fine. My sobs subside and shock descends upon me, leaving a numb, detached calmness in its wake.

"Try the front door. If the key is in this lock, it can't be in that one." I say, surprised by the level of logic I can show at this moment. I guess shock has its benefits sometimes.

Fiona shoots me a look of pride. She appreciates someone who can be level-headed regardless of the panic emulating around them. Stephen, on the other hand, is a ball of nerves. I can hear him muttering soft expletives to himself as he moves towards the front of the villa.

"We ought to go with him," Fiona takes me by the hand and leads me towards the corner of the building Stephen has disappeared behind. "He's not coping well."

"Shouldn't we call security?" I ask.

"There's no dedicated security on the island. It's only us and the staff here. No alarms. No bodyguards. Barely any CCTV. It only points out towards the water where we arrived."

She's very knowledgeable about our surroundings and I must have shot her a confused glance because she quickly added, "I was considering investing in the hotel when the idea was first floated on the market. That's the bit that turned me off, to be honest. Privacy is important, but not as important as safety."

I can hear Stephen grunting in pain as he repeatedly hits the front door. "My key will turn but the bloody door won't open." His face is pale and I feel for him. This has to be his worst nightmare when working somewhere as remote as this. Surely there must be at least a first aider on site, a defibrillator maybe.

"Should someone call the police?" Fiona asks.

"We need to get inside first and work out what we're dealing with." Replies Stephen.

"We've all seen what we're dealing with." My voice is monotone and I try not to let my mind float back to the image of Lucas hanging from the ceiling. It was obvious to anybody with eyes what had happened and Fiona was right. We should call the police. We should call them immediately.

"A half-hearted report isn't going to help anyone. We need to see exactly what has happened." he replies.

Fiona huffs in irritation at Stephen's resistance to make the call. We both know it's the right thing to do but unfortunately, neither of us knows how to dial out on the landline at the check-in desk, let alone the number for the local emergency services. We have no choice but to follow Stephen's lead on this.

"I'll check the other side of the villa," Fiona offers. She gives my hand a squeeze and leaves me with a frustrated Stephen who's still trying to jimmy the door open.

"Stephen?" I try to cut through his frenzy and take a step towards him. "Stephen," I repeat, placing a hand on his arm to prevent him from hitting the door anymore. His knuckles are red and scratched from the effort. He whirls around to face me and for a moment there's a flash of rage on his face and I'm afraid. I hadn't expected his frustration to turn its attention to me.

"Can you help? Do anything. If you're capable." His words are sharp and cold and I feel tears prick at the corner of my eyes once again, except this time they are for me and not Lucas. Lucas. That's who I've got to focus on now. If there's even the tiniest chance he's still alive, we have to get to him before it's too late.

Moving away from Stephen, I walk back towards the patio doors we first saw Lucas through. There's a window slightly ajar on the first floor. I can see the curtain sticking out between the panels as though Lucas closed it without realising they were there. If I can just get up there, then maybe the fabric is thick enough that it's prevented the lock mechanism from kicking in. I look from the window to my feet. It's not that high up. I just need something I can climb.

"Fiona!" I call to her and she comes running, concern for my well-being on her face. "Can you help me move the table and stack the chairs?" she follows my line of sight and notices the same dusty red fabric

I do.

"You can't be serious, Emma."

"We don't have time to argue about this. The sooner we get in, the sooner Stephen will call the authorities." I don't add that I have a sliver of hope that Lucas will still be breathing in the villa.

Fiona shakes her head and walks away from me. I call after her but get no response. As I'm surveying the distance to the window once again, the sound of shattering glass echoes around us.

"What the bloody hell was that?!" Robert shouts as he lightly jogs towards me, appearing from the shadows. Our voices and movements have carried along the night air. Hopefully, more people will arrive soon to help.

"I found a way in!" calls Fiona and without explaining to Robert what he's about to witness, I move towards her voice. The glass from one of the patio doors lays smashed into pieces all over the floor, and I watch as Fiona picks her way across the shards toward Lucas. She grabs hold of his legs and holds him upwards, trying to relieve the pressure on his neck. She has the same hope that I do. That there's still a chance to save him. By this point though, it's obvious that our hope is nothing more than a fantasy. Lucas is dead. The smell of defecation alone can tell me that. I don't take my eyes off Fiona as I move towards her. Her arms are shaking from the weight of the body and I need her to let go.

She shakes her head at me, not wanting to give up on her hope, as I stand in front of her and gently pull his legs from her grasp. They swing awkwardly between us before coming to a pause.

"It's too late." I explain to her, and she begins to cry. She looks up at him as he hangs down above us but I can't do that. I can't bring myself to look up at his face. A face I was speaking to not many hours ago. A face that I'd watched countless times online. A face that the world will mourn.

If you'd asked me who amongst us that day at the restaurant had been a suicide risk, there's no way I would have picked Lucas. Especially not after hearing the excitement in his voice around his upcoming projects. He was finally going to get the world to take him seriously, finally going to feel as though he'd achieved justice for his grandmother. And now it was all just gone.

Robert's hand is around my waist and Stephen's is on Fiona's shoulders as they guide us out of the villa and back into the fresh air. The four of us stand in silence, our backs turned to Lucas's corpse and we stare out towards the jetty by the restaurant. The surrounding water sways gently in the ocean's tide it's pulled from, and it's hypnotic. Almost healing.

"When are we going home?" Robert asks. The weekend cannot continue after such a tragedy.

"Unless the local police can arrange something, there are no flights due out until Monday." Stephen answers.

"Are you serious?" Robert is infuriated.

"We're a very remote island. It's our number one selling point." There's no pride in Stephen's voice as he announces this fact. His ego has been dampened by the sight of a corpse.

"What about one of the speedboats? Surely we can move to the mainland for the rest of the nights?" Fiona's tears have slowed now. She's being practical again.

"The mainland isn't exactly safe for tourists of your calibre, I'm afraid."

"We can't stay here after this!" Robert gestures behind us without looking directly at Lucas. "For Christ's sake, we've at least got to cut him down."

"Stop!" orders Stephen. "We need to wait for the police to give us instructions. They might need us to take photographs of the scene or something before we disturb the body."

The body. That's what Lucas's been reduced to. Nothing more than a body.

"They won't need photographs. It's not a crime scene." I offer, hoping this will force Stephen to see our point of view. We can't just leave him hanging up there. It's not right. We need to at least lay him on the floor so he can rest.

"You can wait for whoever you like but I'm going to do the right thing." announces Robert before taking a deep breath and heading back into the villa. Exchanging a nod with Fiona, we both follow him whilst Stephen stands haplessly on the patio.

Once again Fiona wraps her arms around Lucas's legs, only this time I'm by her side helping. The scent of Lucas's body seeps into my nose and I'm sure I'll never be able to smell anything else.

"Can you hurry, please?" asks Fiona as we watch Robert look around the room. He walks into the open-plan kitchen and we listen as he opens and closes drawers.

"I need to find something to cut the rope." He explains. Fiona sighs and looks at me. As much as we want to do right by Lucas and his family, we don't want to be holding this corpse any longer than we have to. "You could let him go and help me look."

He was right. There was no need for us to be supporting the body until Robert was ready to cut it down. We weren't thinking logically. We thought somehow, by holding him up, we were helping. It was an emotional decision. One that didn't make a lick of sense. My cheeks flushed with embarrassment and I let go of Lucas's legs. The best way to help Lucas right now was to help Robert.

Fiona stayed standing in the living room, her eyes fixed in horror on Lucas's face. I still haven't been able to look at it. I don't want that image seared on my mind. Just as I turn the corner to the kitchen, I hear a shout of success from Robert and he walks past me into the living room with a large kitchen knife. Its pristine surface glimmered in the moonlight that was peeping through the smashed garden doors.

He stands next to Fiona, but rather than having his attention fixed on Lucas, he glances at the room around us. As I'm trying to work out what he's searching for, he walks back into the kitchen wordlessly. He's a man on a mission and by limiting his words, he's able to do what he needs to do. Or perhaps he's just starred in so many horror films he's telling his brain this is a scene. Whatever the reason for his silence, I was grateful for it. There weren't any right words for this moment. None that would suffice.

Once again, he walks past me, back into the living room, this time holding a kitchen stool. Of course. He needed something to stand on to cut the rope. Lucas was suspended high above even Robert's head. He couldn't cut the knot if he couldn't reach it.

With a nod at us both, he climbs up onto the stool and reaches out for the rope. Grasping out for it, the movement causes Lucas's body to sway. It's horrifying to see and I quickly reach out for his legs to stop him. With a clear of his throat, Stephen is at my side, his hands wrapping themselves around the other side of the corpse. Fiona is still rooted to the ground, staring at Lucas's face.

"Fiona, you'll have to support his back as he comes down. Can you do that?" Robert asks.

This question snaps her out of her trance and she takes a step forward, hands outstretched towards Lucas's armpits. Ready to catch him as he comes down to earth for the last time. I can't hold back the tears that are streaming down my face as Robert cuts the rope and we carry Lucas's weight between us. I shush his silent body as though that will bring him comfort. Nothing can bring him comfort anymore, but I hope he's at least at peace now. Laying him on the floor, we stand around him, nobody wanting to break the eerie silence that has descended on the room.

Stephen is the first to speak. "I'll go call the authorities." He doesn't wait for a response before he turns and leaves the villa. I watch him retreat, shoulders heavy with the weight of what has happened under his watch. I make a mental note to talk to him soon, to let him know that this isn't his fault. This is an anomaly he couldn't have planned for. You can't plan for the darkest decisions someone's mind can take them to, you just can't. It took me a long time to accept that truth. Hopefully, the fact that Lucas was a guest and not a friend will help Stephen accept that truth quicker than I did.

My mind fell back to two years ago, the year I turned thirty. The year I found my friend in the same position as Lucas. I'd been on my own when I found her. I was supposed to join her for dinner that night but had been delayed at the last minute due to a work deadline I barely met. Promising to come over for drinks as soon as I finished, I'd taken her lack of response as sulking on her part. I'd turned up two hours late with a bottle of Prosecco and a box of her favourite biscuits to win her over, knowing that within half an hour she'd have forgiven me and we'd be sat on the sofa ignoring a movie and chatting shit. That didn't happen though. The paramedic who attended tried to reassure me that there had been nothing I could do, that she'd been dead for an hour by the time I arrived. It didn't help though. If I had just arrived on time, then I could have talked her out of it. I know I could have.

I glance around the villa looking for a note. My friend had left one so it stood to reason that Lucas would have too. It's only now that I notice the state of the villa.

Paperwork is lying all over the place. His suitcase seems to have been unpacked in a frenzy. Perhaps if I'd had a chance to see his room before dinner, I would have picked up on these clues. The reality behind the mask he presented. They do say that sometimes people who are a danger to themselves are happiest before they take their own lives. And Lucas had seemed happy. Excited even. It all made sense now.

Robert picks the stool up that he'd used and returns it to the kitchen. Silently he returns to me and Fiona and nods. It's time for us to leave. We can't do anything more for Lucas.

Something is niggling at my brain though, as we walk up the path away from his villa. Maybe it's the idea of leaving him alone. I have to remind myself that he's long gone, he doesn't need us anymore.

But still, there's a part of my brain that's crying out to me. Telling me something isn't right. As the three of us split up, still without words, and I walk back towards my room it hits me.

If Robert had to fetch a stool to cut Lucas down, how did Lucas get up there in the first place?

Chapter Eleven

I don't remember the walk back to my room.

Once I'd connected the dots about the kitchen stool, my mind went blank. Sitting on my bed trying to weigh up the implications of what I had realised; there had to be an explanation for this. Perhaps Robert had missed a chair or something that Lucas must have used to tie the rope to the beams before he kicked it out from under himself. Yes. That had to be it.

I close my eyes and try to picture the villa as we found it, but all I can picture is the wide open space beneath Lucas. I can't bring up the memory of any overturned furniture nearby that he could have used. I guess in the moment's madness I wasn't looking for it and therefore can't remember it.

Yes, that's it.

Trauma is playing with my memory. Although my body is exhausted and mildly hungover already, my brain won't let me entertain the idea of sleep. At least not yet.Picking through the pile of towels where I'd left it, I find my old digital camera.

If I have photographs, then my mind can't start imagining things that were or weren't there. I need evidence of the scene the way we found it, if only to keep myself sane. I know what this is. It's me trying desperately to find any other reason for what happened to Lucas than accepting that he made the choice himself. I'd done it briefly when I found my friend. Certain there would be somebody else in the house who'd hurt her, it's why I'd hidden when I'd called the police. Just in case the perpetrator wanted to hurt me too. But there had been no one else in that house other than my friend's illness and there wasn't some nefarious villain on this island. I was trying to excuse away the truth, and at least with photographs, I'd have something concrete that could stop me from wandering down that mental path.

I've never seen a night sky so dark as the one I step out into. With no light pollution around, there was nothing but the stars and the moon to guide my way as I walked as quietly as I could back towards Lucas's villa. The police would arrive soon and I wanted my fellow guests to get as much sleep as they could before their weekend was interrupted. I wish I knew which villas were Fiona's or Robert's. It would be good to have some company right now. Then again, if what happened to Lucas wasn't straightforward, I should probably keep my suspicions to myself. I couldn't know who was responsible.

No, Emma. Stop turning this into something this isn't. Go to the villa. Take your photos and put your doubts at ease.

The shattered glass on the patio floor glimmers in the moonlight and a shiver runs down my spine. I should turn back and try to sleep. Nothing good can come of this. Everything will seem more logical in the morning without shock and alcohol clouding my judgement. And yet my feet keep moving towards the garden doors. I have to look, if only to settle my imagination. Pausing to take a photo of the smashed door, I curse myself for forgetting that I need to use the flash on my camera in this light. It's bound to attract attention and then I'll be in trouble.

Although, in the grand scheme of events that have occurred tonight, smuggling a contraband camera onto the island isn't the most worrying. I stand still and listen to the world around me to see if anyone has noticed the sudden flash of the camera but thankfully the air is silent. I'm still alone.

I walk into the living room and grimace at Lucas's body. His eyes are cloudy and blank; his expression is unreadable. I could have happily gone the rest of my life without seeing another dead body, let alone one in such similar circumstances. Against the moral voice in my head, I snap a few photos of Lucas's body. The marks around his neck, the scratches on his arm. It will all help me build a picture of what happened here. This was a tragedy. Nothing more. Nothing less.

Standing up from my kneeling position, I look around the body. Just as I'd remembered, there was no overturned furniture nearby. I take a photograph of the scene as bile rises in my throat. Something definitely isn't right here. There's no logical way Lucas could have tied himself to the beams. But if he didn't do it, then who did?

Moving away from Lucas, I take photos of the disarray around him. The open suitcase and scattered papers. It's almost as if he'd been looking for something before he died. Or somebody was searching after he did. The shiver returns to my spine. I need to get out of this villa. I need to go to bed and in the morning this will all have been a dream.

I reach down towards one scrap of torn-up notebook paper. It has Michael's name scrawled upon it. This must have been the evidence Lucas was talking about. These were his case notes. I pick up another scrap of paper and nearly drop it out of shock. Penny's name is on it, underlined three times.

No. This is too much for me. I'm not supposed to see this. I need to leave before I get myself into any more trouble. I drop both scraps of paper to the floor and stand. Part of me wants to keep rooting through the chaos on the floor around me, to see what else I can find. See if I can find any further explanation or, God forbid, any more names. But the journalistic part of me knows that if you go looking for trouble, you will always find it, and right now I just want to be safely sequestered back in my room. I've done what I came here to do. I've taken my pictures and proved my anxiety right. I don't need to make this mystery any worse.

Just as I'm making my way past the body towards the patio, I hear voices approaching. Shit.

Nervously I glance around to see if there's anywhere for me to hide but unfortunately for me the downstairs of the villa is open plan and short of hiding behind the sofa, I have no hope of staying out of view.

Quickly, I place my camera into the pockets of the shorts I'm wearing under my dress. My mum always used to tease me about it but to this day I wear shorts under any dress or skirt. Even cycle shorts when I dared to wear something tight. There was something about the possibility of my underwear being exposed to the world that just didn't sit right with me. That and the unpleasant rubbing sensation one can get between your thighs on a hot and sweaty day.

It wasn't the world's smallest camera though, and I was conscious of the bulge through the fabric of my dress. The voices were now coming up the path towards the smashed door, male and female. Stephen and Sam most likely. They were probably leading the police to the scene and here I was acting like a guilty party. I just had to hope that when the inspectors noticed what I had, they would believe my alibi. I had been with the rest of the group for the entire evening and then spent time alone with Fiona. My every movement could be accounted for, but could I say the same for my fellow travellers?

Before paranoia could fester too long in my brain, I plop myself down onto the sofa, hoping that the camera will be less obvious in a sitting position. I look at Lucas's body and once again, hot tears prick at the corners of my eyes, but this time they are tears of fear. Fear of the fact I may have stumbled across something that was better left alone.

"Emma?" Stephen's voice is steady as he takes a step towards me and I avert my gaze from his. I've never been the world's best liar. It's why I'd repeated my cover story for this weekend to myself hundreds of times. Dad always said how easy my honesty made my childhood but it certainly played havoc with my adulthood. There are just some times in life it pays to be a skilled liar. And this was going to be one of them.

"Oh, Stephen. Hi." I take pauses between my words, wanting them to sound disjointed, needing to put across the real shock coursing through my veins. "I didn't want to leave Lucas alone."

"You shouldn't be here by yourself." Sam's words were gentler than I'd expected and she sat down next to me on the sofa whilst Stephen regarded the body. "We're here now. We can take care of this."

"When are the police coming? Will I have to give a statement?" I want to speak to them before anybody else. Before they piece together the mystery themselves. That will look better for me than admitting at a later date that I had suspicions of my own.

"They're going to get here as soon as they can –"

"Unfortunately, the water is rather treacherous between here and the mainland and they don't have anything more modern than a few speed boats. It could be tomorrow." Stephen cuts Sam off with his statement.

"Tomorrow?!" I try to keep the exasperation from my tone but I can't help it. We can't be expected to carry on as usual knowing that Lucas is lying here, dead. The police need to get here tonight whilst everything is intact.

"They've asked us to store the body for them. It's supposed to be a very hot day tomorrow." Stephen says, explaining the reason for his upcoming actions.

A tightness rises from my stomach, gripping its way around my throat. I know exactly what the police are implying. They don't want him to rot. They need to preserve the body for the sake of his family.

"Don't worry. We'll take care of everything. The kitchen staff are on their way to help and we'll make sure the villa is closed off." Sam has her hand under my arm and is helping me to my feet. All worries of them noticing the camera have slipped from my mind at their explanation of what is going to happen here tonight. What they're going to do with Lucas. Where are they going to store him? How long will he be kept there? What are the other guests going to say when the news is broken to them?

I let Sam guide me out of the villa and I thank her before picking my way back down the path to my accommodation. Back in England, the police would never ask witnesses to store a body themselves. They'd certainly never let the scene of a death be tampered with and traipsed over. But I guess that way of thinking is small-minded, just because they do things a certain way back home, doesn't mean they have to do the same in other places. Rich people places. They do things differently here because things are different here. I just have to trust that when the police finally arrive, they'll listen to my worries. And if they don't, at least I have photographic evidence they won't be able to deny.

Sitting down on my bed, my brain finally agrees to let me rest. I've done what it asked of me. I went and checked the scene and unfortunately found something unpleasant. But staying awake worrying about it won't help anyone. It was better to get a little rest and to start the morning with a more logical, sober mindset. Feeling paranoid, I place my camera under my pillow, knowing it will remain there safe and undiscovered until morning. Everything will look better when the sun rises. I was sure of it.

Yet when I turn the light out and climb under the covers, all I can picture is Lucas's villa. The living room is devoid of any overturned furniture. Lucas's body hanging from an impossibly high position.

His excitement as he shared his upcoming work with me on the jetty. His warning to me about being careful. He had told me that the people I was surrounded with were capable of deeds I couldn't imagine. But surely he didn't mean out-and-out murder.

Nobody here was capable of that. If I was in the presence of a killer, I'd know. The hairs on my arms would stand to attention or I'd have unexplained anxiety as my body responded on instinct to their presence. Surely. My survival instinct would kick in to let me know that something about someone wasn't right. That had to be true. Because if it wasn't, then I was left with one horrible fact.

I am stuck in paradise with a murderer.

Chapter Twelve

I try to keep my eyes closed for as long as possible, enjoying the fluffy comfort of the luxury mattress enveloping my body.

The covers are the lightest cotton that's ever touched my skin and for a moment I've forgotten everything that happened last night. Everything in the world is okay and I'm looking forward to spending the day living the high life by the pool with Fiona. For a moment, my mind slips back to the seconds before our lips touched. I can smell her perfume all around. She smelled like an old book. Not in a musty way. There was no scent of moss or mildew about her. It was warm and inviting. It reminded me of the local library I had loved so much as a child. If you're a reader, you'll know the exact scent I mean, it grows up your nose and warms your heart, holding out the prospect of adventure and mysteries. That's what Fiona smelt like - adventure and mystery. It was intoxicating.

Then she'd leant forward, her face millimetres from mine. I can assure you that there is no hint of a wrinkle or a surgery scar upon her skin. It's unblemished and it gleamed in the moonlight and I knew that if I reached out to touch her face, it would be the most supple thing my fingertips had ever caressed. Forget the wine. The attraction was intoxicating enough. I still couldn't quite believe that she'd taken an interest in me, but I wasn't about to turn down a chance at happiness because of my self-deprecation. So I'd chosen her over Robert. Something teenage me would never, **ever** forgive me for. But I'd rather live with childish regrets than lose out on the chance to get to know such a phenomenal woman.

Her lips were soft against mine and her tongue was gentle. She'd used just the right amount of pressure. It was a kiss that promised of things to come. Then we'd pulled apart. I'd looked over her shoulder and –

A scream freezes in my throat and my eyes spring open at the memory. I wish we'd never broken our kiss. I wish we'd chosen a different route back to her villa. I wish we hadn't been the ones to find Lucas. If we hadn't discovered him, then we'd both be waking up blissfully unaware together in Fiona's bed. We'd at least have these few hours before breakfast when Stephen would break the news to us. We'd be horrified, of course, but at least we wouldn't have the trauma of all we lived through last night. Suddenly I'm painfully aware of the smell of death lingering around me, unsurprising really, given I'd been holding a dead body six hours ago.

With a shudder, I throw the cover off myself and strip my pyjamas off. Thankfully I'd packed spares as I know I won't want to wear these ever again. Even if I boiled them clean, they'd still reek of a night I'd rather forget. I push them down into the kitchen bin and walk through to the bathroom in just my underwear. As I turn the taps on to run a bath, I wrap a large towel around myself - just in case any unexpected visitors decide to call round. Closing the bathroom door, I'm relieved to find a lock on it and as I bolt it closed, I finally feel the blanket of safety wrap itself around me. Closing the toilet lid, I take a seat and watch as the steam from the water rises up from the porcelain tub. Even though I have the photos to look back at, I still can't believe I was right about Lucas's villa. He hadn't hung himself.

He couldn't have. There is a slim chance that he convinced somebody to help him end his life but given that everyone here was a virtual stranger to each other, that's unlikely. It's unlikely that he'd ask and it's unlikely that anyone would accept. But it is a possibility, however small, that I can't discount. And it's a far more pleasant possibility than the one that came to me just as sleep took me for the night. That there's a killer in our midst.

As I sink into the hot water, my muscles unleash the tension I've held in my body since seeing Lucas through that door. Now I was fully awake, I could logically talk myself out of taking any further trips down memory lane. Thinking about lost friends and rehashing old guilt wouldn't do a single thing to help me right now. Those were all words I could share with my mum when I got home later today. I can't wait to fall into her arms and for her to make everything okay again. No matter how old I get, I think I'm always going to want my mum when things get too hard in life. It's an instinctual bond between us.

I wash my body, taking my time to methodically scrub away the feeling of dead flesh from my own. My hands are red and raw by the time I'm finished but I don't wince in pain. They have to be clean. I have to be clean. If I'm clean, then it's like it never happened - like it was all a terrible nightmare. That's what I tell myself, even though I know it isn't true.

That's the problem with being a terrible liar. I can't even lie to myself when I need it most. There are many truths about this situation I am avoiding whilst lying in the bathtub. The truth is, Lucas is dead. The truth is he couldn't have acted alone, even if he was willing. The truth is, my hands may never feel clean again. Eventually, the water will grow cold and I will have to face the world outside. I will have to listen as Stephen tells everyone over breakfast about what happened last night. At least I won't be alone then. I'll have other people around me and that, I'm sure, will make the whole situation more bearable.

I won't lie to you, as I pull out the plug and let the water drain around me, there's one person in particular I want to see more than anyone. And it isn't Fiona. The one person I want to see most in the world right now is Michael. If, and I do mean if, Lucas's death wasn't at his own hands, then the former politician is my most likely suspect. Lucas was planning an exposé that would ruin Michael's entire life and blossoming celebrity career. Even the best spin doctors in the industry wouldn't be able to weasel him out of that scandal.

Growing up, my friends used to tell me that I'd always sniff out a story whether there was one or not. That I'd find trouble if I rooted through something long enough. It wasn't the case here on the island though. Something was wrong, I was sure of it. Try as I might, I just couldn't imagine a feasible situation in which someone here would help a stranger take their own life. No. Something much darker was afoot at Hotel Horizen, and as a fledgling journalist, it was my duty to follow the clues. I'd get to the bottom of who killed Lucas and that will be the story that launches my career. Not some fluff piece about rich versus poor. My words on this case will matter to the world, because the world will mourn Lucas's passing. Of that I am sure. You can't be such a huge part of culture and expect it not to miss you when you're gone.

By now I've towelled off and am standing in front of the open suitcase laid out on my bed. Why didn't I bring anything black with me? Over half my wardrobe at home is black and it seems the most appropriate colour to wear today. Oh yes, I know why all I brought with me were neutrals and pastels. I wanted to blend in and when I'd been packing for this trip, all the articles on capsule wardrobes I'd read focused on various shades of beige and white.

A way to look effortlessly chic, whatever the circumstances. Unless someone died, then you're just left feeling tacky. I settle for an oversized shirt in the darkest shade of beige I can find and a large pair of dark sunglasses. This is going to have to do and at least it will hide the red rings around my eyes. I spritz some leave-in conditioner through my hair and pull it up into a ponytail. I should make more of an effort with my appearance, given I'm still playing the part. But all I want to do is get down to the restaurant for breakfast and witness how Michael reacts to the news of Lucas's death.

As I pull the door behind me, I'm struck again by another oddity from last night. Lucas's villa door was locked and yet mine didn't even appear to have a keyhole. Is my room just unfinished or did Lucas request an additional layer of security upon checking in? That wouldn't surprise me, given the notes I found in his room. He probably wouldn't want Michael or Penny - that's right, I'd almost forgotten finding Penny's name amongst the chaos - stumbling across his evidence against them. But yes, that must be the explanation. He must have demanded a villa with extra security to protect whatever it was he was working on from prying eyes.

I'm taken aback to find Fiona sitting on the stone edging that surrounds the flowers by my villa's entrance. There are two mugs by her feet and she's watching the steam rise from them. Her hair, which had seemed so loose and free yesterday, is now pulled back into a large bun and most of her face is obscured by her comically large black sunglasses. It looks like I'm not the only one trying to hide the effects of last night. Finally, she notices me and picks up both mugs as she stands. She holds one out towards me.

"I thought you might want a little pre-breakfast caffeine." She smiles at me but due to the sunglasses, I can't see if it makes it to her eyes.

Of course, she packed a black dress. Granted, it was a maxi dress with deep cuts at the sides but I should have known better than to assume a few hastily read articles could show me how the 1% really dress. Once again I felt self-conscious about my appearance but tried to shrug it off as I had bigger fish to fry.

"Thank you." I take a grateful sip and we start walking slowly towards the restaurant.

"How did you sleep?" she asks.

"Terribly. You?"

"Same."

She lets out a deep sigh and taps her nails absentmindedly against the mug she's holding in both hands. The urge to confide my worries in her overwhelms me.

"Fiona, I don't think what happened last night is what it seems." I need her to push me to explain myself. I don't want to risk sounding like a crazy person without her at least having an interest in what I have to say.

"I don't think so either." She agrees ominously and I'm shocked. I want to stop our walk and grill her on her paranoias to see if they complement mine. But before I can find the words to respond, Stephen pops his head out of the restaurant doors and waves us over. It's showtime.

Chapter Thirteen

Stephen looks exhausted as he holds the door open for us. I imagine he's been on the phone most of the night with the police and the managers of the resort. He must have been asked so many questions he doesn't have the answers to, and I feel genuine empathy towards him. I nod my head at him ever so briefly in a sign of camaraderie but it's as though he looks straight through me with empty eyes as he pulls the door to a close behind us.

Penny is sitting nursing a cup of coffee, quietly nibbling at a triangle of toast. Michael is leaning back in his chair, surveying his full breakfast plate with anticipation. He's obviously made the most of the chefs in the kitchen this morning, and who can blame him? As far as he's, at least outwardly, concerned, we have a beautiful day of lazing around ahead of us, so why not start with a full stomach? Or perhaps killing Lucas caused his appetite to grow.

I almost want to tell Stephen to wait to break the news until the two of them have had a chance to enjoy the morning. There's no sense in them wasting their last few hours in paradise in the same way Robert, Fiona and I will. Speaking of Robert, he's sitting at a table towards the back of the room. Three mugs of coffee on the table. He gestures us over to him and Michael doesn't hide his curiosity at the creation of our little group. For a moment, it looks as though he might get up and join us, but he thinks better of it and picks up his knife and fork.

Stephen is still standing by the front doors and gently clears his throat, turning all attention to him. My body stiffens as I fight the urge to cause a distraction, to delay his announcement even by a minute.

I want to find out what Fiona meant when she agreed with my suspicions, to learn what she thinks she knows. I want to check in with Robert and see how he's coping. I want to do both of these things before I have to cope with any further reactions to the tragic death of Lucas. And yet there's a part of me that's on edge because I'm desperate for Stephen to speak his words.

Because I want to watch Penny and Michael as he does. I want to keep my eye out for any kind of sign of their innocence. Or their guilt. I'm hoping that they're as terrible liars as I am. That I can take their emotions at face value. The only problem with that hope is that they are successful people. And, at least in my experience, people don't achieve their levels of success without a solid poker face.

"Last night I'm afraid something happened. Lucas Jones sadly passed away." Stephen says.

That's it. He doesn't expand on the details of the situation, not yet anyway. I study Penny and Michael, who have both placed their hands palm down on the table. Mugs of coffee and large breakfasts forgotten. Penny's jaw is tight and the bottom lid of her eyes are glassy, but tears aren't spilling. The colour has completely drained from Michael's face and his eyes are darting around the room as though searching for hidden cameras.

"How?" asks Penny. Her voice quivers slightly but still, her face gives nothing away.

"It seems Mr Jones may have been suffering from depression, and he chose last night to, well, not suffer any longer." Stephen spoke with the clumsiness of someone who's never had a loved one suffer from the black pit that can be mental health problems. Never lost someone he loved in such a painful way. Suicide was never the answer. It is never the answer. And yet Stephen is painting it as a reasonable conclusion to Lucas's problems. Problems I'm not even sure existed.

Michael lets out a small gasp as one of his hands flies to his mouth. Either this man had big emotions or he was trying his best to show the world what he deemed to be a normal reaction to this news. I didn't find it too suspicious. I'd seen many a press conference with him where he came across as a robot trying to seem human. Laughing too hard at a journalist's quip or straining to bring tears to his eyes when discussing the fire at the care home. Michael was just a politician. That didn't make him a murderer though.

Penny was the one I was more interested in. She may have been the one to ask for more details, but so far she had made no show of having heard Stephen's reply. There was no gentle nod of the head or sympathetic cluck - the one she'd wheeled out in many celebrity interviews I'd watched. She isn't playing the part now, and I'm not sure why. Surely this is exactly when she should reel out her most empathetic persona? To prove to us she's just as kind as the camera makes her out to be. But she's not bothered about appearances in the face of this news and I can't work out why.

I'm not sure what I expected either of them to do. To stand up proudly and declare that it was one of them who ended Lucas's life? For guilt to overtake them so totally that they combusted? Whatever it was that I was expecting, the show in front of me was not it. I was still no clearer on where I should point my suspicions. The only thing I knew for certain was that I could at least trust Fiona and Robert. I'd been with the two of them for the entire night, from the moment we arrived at dinner until the minute we discovered Lucas's body.

Or, at least, I suppose I'd been with Fiona for all of that time. Robert had retired to his villa alone after I opted to stay and enjoy Fiona's company. But we only sat by the pool for another twenty minutes after he left, hadn't we? It was hard to say without my phone to keep track of time. The only watch I'd ever worn had been my step counter and I hadn't thought to bring that on holiday with me. I didn't need the little vibrations of guilt every hour, reminding me I wasn't moving enough.

However long it had been, surely it hadn't been enough time to murder somebody and stage a crime scene? No, I was certain of Roberts's innocence.

Penny and Michael, on the other hand, had no alibi, however. Michael had excused himself from dinner as soon as it ended and had plenty of time, and motive, to hide away in Lucas's villa waiting for his return. Penny had stormed off soon after Robert and I had joined her and Fiona for after-dinner drinks by the pool. It didn't give her as much time to have acted as Michael may have had, but I couldn't discount the fact I found her name on a scrap of paper in Lucas's room as well.

"The police will be here as soon as they can make it in from the mainland. Crossing the water can be a little difficult at times." Stephen explains. Although there isn't a cloud in the sky to be seen, we are an hour away from the mainland, so maybe it's a different story weather-wise in their port. "Of course, they will want to speak to us all on arrival but until then, they suggested we carry on as normal. The area surrounding Mr Jones's villa is off-limits but nothing is preventing you from enjoying the rest of the facilities we have on offer."

Robert lets out a snort of derision, which Stephen cuts off with a sharp look. I don't blame Robert though, the last thing I feel like doing right now is sunbathing by the pool. It would be disrespectful.

"And what would you suggest as an alternative, Mr. Castro? That we all stay in our villas and mourn a man that, frankly, you all barely knew?" Stephens's voice is cold; a sliver of anger cuts through his tone. There's no customer service cushion around his words. As though he's personally offended by the empathy we're showing for Lucas's passing. He's not wrong. We barely knew Lucas. But he was still one of us. Someone who was supposed to be enjoying a weekend of decadence, not someone who deserved to be strung up to die.

Happy he has calmed Roberts's derision, Stephen continues. "As I was saying. All the facilities are open, our staff are on hand should you need anything and I will be sure to check in on each of you privately today to share any updates on the situation. And, of course, to see how you're coping." This time he turns his gaze to Michael, who's still as white as a ghost. He hasn't made a noise since his initial gasp of shock at the news. It's as though he's barely with us in the room.

Having made his announcement, Stephen flounces from the room, leaving the rest of us in various levels of stunned silence. Robert, Fiona, and I finish our now cold coffees and without exchanging a word, stand simultaneously and move toward the door.

"Tell me you aren't going for a swim." Penny's tone was unreadable. Was she trying to make a dark joke or did she believe we were off to enjoy ourselves?

"I think we all need something a little stronger than coffee this morning," replies Fiona. It's not quite an invitation nor is it an exclusion. But thankfully for my mindset, Michael and Penny do not stand to join us. I need some time away from them to put the pieces together in my mind, settle my paranoia, and maybe even confide in my new friends. There's nothing like trauma bonding to speed along a new friendship into firmer territory.

We leave the restaurant and walk towards the nearest bar in unison, our steps syncing poetically with each other. I was safe with them, I could confide in them my fears and hopefully, Fiona would do the same. She had alluded to her suspicions before we'd been hailed inside the restaurant by Stephen.

"I don't see why the police aren't here already," began Fiona as Robert made his way behind the mahogany bar and began rooting through the back shelves. He held up a bottle of tequila and Fiona shook her head, "It's 10 a.m., Robert."

"You heard what Stephen said, the weather is making it difficult for them to get to us." he replies with his back turned to us. His shoulders were tight with stress, which only increased how good they looked under his shirt.

No, Emma. Now is not the time for those thoughts. You aren't thirteen anymore, you're thirty-two and you need to act your age. It's tough, though, when you've been sleeping alone for a year to not notice how attractive the movie star standing in front of you is.

Fiona makes an unimpressed noise of understanding as she leans over the bar and picks up three glasses that are lying on the drying board just next to the sink. Right on cue, Robert turns back to us with a bottle of vodka in one hand and a carton of orange juice in another.

"A breakfast drink," he offers with a smile as he pours the liquids into each of the glasses. He moves back round to the front of the bar and sits down next to Fiona. She momentarily leans her head on his shoulder and I can't help the pang of jealousy that seeps through me.

"So, how long have you two known each other?" I try to keep my question light, not wanting them to know how interested I was in the answer.

"Childhood friends. Our parents used to socialise with each other." Fiona explains with no further information, as though that was enough of an answer. And she was right, annoyingly so. They didn't owe me any further explanation after all.

"So, what did you mean when we were walking to the restaurant? You don't think Lucas's death is quite what it seems?" she asks me.

"No, I don't, and neither do you." I reply. I'm not going to give her the chance to change her story now that Robert was with us. I needed her to be on the same side as me. She nods and now leans towards me, her head hanging low as though she's about to tell me a secret. But before she can confide in me, Robert interrupts.

"You're being ridiculous. These things, unfortunately, happen all the time around the world. Even in paradise, one can't escape their own mind." Roberts's dismissal is as true as it is patronising. Depression can hunt a person anywhere in the world, but it wasn't depression that killed Lucas. The more time I spent thinking about it, the more I was certain.

"Robert. If Lucas hung himself, how did he climb up to the beam to tie the rope?" Fiona asks the question that's been plaguing me.

"He probably used a chair," answers Robert, certain of himself.

"You had to find something to climb on to cut him down, though, didn't you?" she asks.

She's leading him towards the truth the two of us already share. If we can get him on board, then we'll be safer. It will be the three of us against the two suspects. The police are bound to listen to us if we all have the same anomaly to point out.

The tan drains from Robert's face as he replays the memory of cutting Lucas down from the ceiling. Of his stress levels as he searched the villa for a stool to stand on that would allow him to be the right height for the rope. Of putting it back into the kitchen once the deed was done.

"Shit." He says.

Chapter Fourteen

Robert sits silently and I watch as the cogs in his mind wrap themselves around the truth presented to him. Then, as though a piece of fabric has gotten caught amongst his brain's inner workings, his face drops. It's expressionless. His eyes are blank.

"There has to be an explanation." he mutters before snapping back to reality. Some things are too painful to accept. Or in this case, too terrifying to contemplate. If we're right, if Lucas didn't kill himself, then we have much bigger problems right now than when the police will arrive.

If the killer realises we're onto them, they might behave rashly. They might lash out to keep their secret buried. A shiver runs up my spine and I look over my shoulder. I can feel eyes upon my skin but I see nobody around.

"You know what the explanation is, Castro." She calls him by his surname, a sign of familiarity between them. A way to get him to accept the truth of the matter.

"Are you suggesting someone on this island had something to do with it?" he asks.

"How much do you know about them? The others, I mean." I ask suddenly, nearly cutting over Robert's question.

I can't help interjecting. My journalistic instincts have kicked in and I need to gather evidence, opinions, and statements. I need to build a picture of those on this island so I can better protect myself.

"Penny and Michael? Only what I've seen on the news. And it's not exactly like Michael has gone international. The only reason I know his name is the effect his sacking had on the British economy." replies Fiona. Of course, she doesn't pay attention to UK news unless it directly affects her business. Why should she care about some small-time politician's attempt to rise through the social echelons?

"The same, pretty much. I've met Penny a few times at premieres and parties..." Robert pauses, alluding to the fact he has more of a story but isn't quite willing to share. It's a clever technique to make sure the surrounding interest is focused on you before a big reveal.

"Well, she certainly doesn't seem to be a fan of yours." I raise my eyebrows as I state the obvious.

"That may have something to do with her wife. I slept with her. Twice." he replies, looking bashful. Attempting to channel his inner naughty schoolboy to lessen his moral crimes.

"ROBERT!" exclaims Fiona, her face genuinely contorted in disgust. "Twice! Christ, if I were her you'd be six feet under by now." Her hand flies to her mouth as soon as the words leave her tongue. Now isn't the time for jokes like that.

Robert's revelation has me worried for that exact reason though. If Penny was willing to kill Lucas for writing some kind of exposé on her, what fate would she bestow upon the man who disrespected her marriage?

"It takes two." Robert defended himself to Fiona.

"You never could make a mistake just once, could you?"

There's a glint in her eye as she speaks. History laced into her barb that I have no knowledge of.

"I thought we were past that?" Robert replies, matching the intensity in her features. It's as though they've forgotten I'm present, forgotten the whole reason we're sitting out here alone.

"I think we need-" I interject. Hoping to get us back on track.

"She was my best friend, Bobby. You don't get past something like that. Not really." Fiona snarls.

"I told you back then how sorry I was. I never meant to hurt Catherine." Robert defends.

"Well, you did. And I hurt her when I kept you in my life. Do you know how long it's been since I've seen her?"

"No." Robert's tone is flat. He knows the question was rhetorical.

"Six years. Six years without my best friend, Robert. Because of your stupid mistakes."

"I never asked you to choose me."

"I didn't choose you." Her voice drops as she finishes her sentence. "I just didn't choose her."

The two of them turn away from each other, not quite like children, but not that far from it. The pain between them is tangible and I'm not sure how to handle this situation. On one hand, I should let sleeping dogs lie. Wait for their exchange to lose its sting and attempt to regroup later on in the day when we've all had a little space. On the other hand, we might have a murderer in our midst.

Fiona makes my choice for me as she stands, glass in hand. Wordlessly, she picks up the vodka bottle, forgoing the orange juice, and tops her drink to the brim.

"I'm going for a walk." she announces and without waiting for a reply or any pushback, she walks away from us. Something tingles in my gut as I watch her saunter off. Splitting up is a bad idea. We need to stick together. There's safety in numbers.

Robert sighs and shakes his head. He's watching her disappear into the distance just as I am. I wonder if he has the same reservations as I do, but as I'm about to ask him, he speaks.

"Shit." He rubs his hands across his face. Before his argument with Fiona, I would have noticed how attractive a movement this was. But now that I knew more about the man he was, he had lost his gleam. Never meet your heroes and all that.

"She's not wrong. Mistakes are my specialty."

"We all make them." I offer lamely.

"Not you, I imagine. Not like this."

"Well, no. But I'm sure some of my exes might disagree."

He smiles ruefully at my comment. As though it's impossible to him that I too may have broken some hearts along my path in life. But I'm sure I have. Statistically speaking, we all have, whether we meant to or not.

I cheated on Christine with Simon. That was the truth of it. I hadn't been shy about it either. I purposefully sprayed his aftershave on my jacket as I snuck out of his flat and returned to my bed with her. I left my phone unlocked in the hopes she'd find his messages. I was too much of a coward to break up with her myself, I needed her to call time. And I suppose, there was a part of me that loved the drama of it all. I was so certain she'd catch on to my betrayal, my cheeks flushed every time I lied to her. She knew that was my tell. And yet she kept any suspicions to herself. Until she could no longer bury her head in the sand. Until one of our mutual friends caught me in Simon's arms. She couldn't cope with the embarrassment of publicly forgiving me and thankfully she left our flat the very same day.

Simon hadn't known about Christine. Well, he knew of her existence but he'd just assumed she was my roommate. I never told him otherwise, not even in the nine months we openly dated. I guess in a way I'd cheated on him too, at least for the first month. Eventually, I broke his heart too. Left him to concentrate on myself. Thought life would somehow be more fulfilling and exciting without his steady presence. And it had, at least for a while. I couldn't tell Robert any of this though, I didn't want to taint the image he had of me. The innocence of me.

"We should probably all stick together, shouldn't we?" I say, hoping he'll agree instantly and we can follow Fiona together. Instead, he smiles at me.

"Look. I get that it's a bit strange, the Lucas thing, and maybe it is more than it seems on the surface level. But it's not like there's a maniac on the loose. For all we know, if this was something more than a suicide, it was someone with a personal vendetta. Lucas Jones wasn't as clean as he liked to make out."

"It is more than it seems Robert. You have to believe me." I push.

"What I have to believe is that anyone in our position in life has left behind a string of enemies. And Lucas had just as many as the rest of us should rumours be believed."

"He was working on something. Something about Michael and Penny." I say, instantly wishing I could take the words back. I hadn't meant to share that spot of information with anyone. It would only lead to questions. The most prominent one being how I knew. Which would lead to me having to explain that I'd been snooping around the crime scene. Which would just make me look guilty and as the outsider of the group, I didn't want to look guilty when the truth about me was revealed.

"He was a creep, Emma. Plain and simple. If he was killed by somebody else, then he finally hit on the wrong girl. And if he killed himself, I can think of numerous reasons why he would have done so," says Robert, ignoring all my interjections.

I'm stunned by Roberts's outburst and have to look away from him as I process it. Lucas had been so kind to me on the jetty, and so excited to be playing the part of Robin Hood against Michael's crimes. Somebody who believed so passionately in righting a wrong couldn't possibly be guilty of what Robert was insinuating.

"I'm just saying, there's a moral difference between liking older girls and liking younger women." He adds, not blind to his own romantic fallacies.

It was undoubtedly true that Lucas's fan base was predominantly made up of teenagers across the age scale, but there had never even been a whisper of what Robert was describing. Not a single hashtag on social media or a thinly veiled jibe in a gossip column. Something like that couldn't occur without someone somewhere talking about it, surely. Why was Robert sharing this with me anyway? Was he trying to cheer me up by letting me know that Lucas was a bad person? Did that mean he deserved to die? No, absolutely not. There's no way Robert would suggest that.

"Please. Can we just find Fiona?" I ask. Trying to change the subject and reunite myself with the people I trusted all in one swoop.

"You can do as you like. I'm going to have another drink." He was frustrated, irritated that his exposé of Lucas hadn't slowed my fear. Because even if he was right, even if Lucas had been killed by someone with a personal vendetta, what's to say they didn't have an issue with anyone else on the island? If what Robert said was true, about leaving a trail of enemies along the path to success, then surely every other guest here might be in danger? And, without doubt, there was no one more successful on this island than Fiona. I had to find her and warn her.

I stand without responding, part of me still believing that he'll follow, but as I walk away from the bar, I hear the slosh of liquid being poured into a glass, and it's clear I'm on my own.

I don't remember the paths in the resort feeling so claustrophobic when I arrived, but now the tropical plants and bushes feel like they're closing in on me. Obscuring me from view. I want to call out Fiona's name but don't want to appear desperate. I'm fine. I'm safe here. There is no need to panic. Breathe in for four. Out for eight. Keep the panic at bay.

Mum always said I had an overactive imagination. She wasn't wrong. When I was a child, every nightmare was shockingly realistic and left me refusing to sleep in my room. I was so sure that the faces I'd seen in the walls were there, hiding. That they were out to get me. Of course, now as an adult, I know they weren't, but that's the problem with lucid dreaming. Everything seems so real. Dad used to make up stories about goblins and fairies when we walked the neighbour's dog through the woods. He stopped eventually though, when I developed a fear of the sweeping trees and the mysteries they could be hiding.

I've grown up since then though. Now I know there are no monstrous faces in the walls preparing to eat me, no fairy-tale creatures hiding in trees, or a hero coming to sweep me off my feet. My imagination, as an adult, now manifests itself in an underlying sense of anxiety. Never quite bad enough to require medication, but loud enough at times to stop me in my tracks. This was one of those times.

There's rustling in the bush ahead of me. Something large, a person, is hiding in them. I can hear their staggered breathing as they try to stay quiet. I try to force words from my throat to call for help, but they're strangled by the tightness rising from my gut. I need to run. No. I can't run. If I run, then they'll know I've spotted them. They might give chase. My best bet is to feign a need to turn on my heel and then casually walk back towards Robert.

Fiona. Fiona came down this path. What if she's the one in the bush and her breathing is staggered because she's injured?

I'm frozen with indecision. On the one hand, danger could be just ahead of me. On the other hand, somebody could need my help. A thought flashes through my mind - I wish I had my phone so I could call my parents. No matter how old or independent I get, I think I'll always think of them as having all the answers. But they aren't here. They can't help me. This decision is mine and mine alone to make.

"Emma?" whispers the bush. It's a man's voice. Not Fiona. Now is the time to run.

"Emma?" it calls again. "You have to help me." Now I recognise the plummy tones. It's Michael. The chief suspect, as far as I'm concerned, in Lucas's death.

I stand still as a statue as he emerges from the bush. Stumbling as he does so. His movements are jerky and his head swivels from side to side as he checks who's around us. In his hand is a notebook, and across his chinos are red splatters. Blood?

"Michael, please," I beg as I take a step back. But he doesn't stop moving towards me. I look around. Other than the pool and the small cabin next to it, there is nowhere to hide. I could turn and run towards Robert, but that would mean turning my back on Michael. And I'm not sure I'm brave enough for that.

"Help me. You have to. It's everywhere." He says, his words are frantic and too fast for his tongue. He slips over some of his pronunciation.

"Leave me alone. Please. Just let me pass."

"Don't know how they did it. Lucas knew. Who else knows? Do you know?" he asks as he takes another step towards me. His pupils are dilated and he chews at his own lip as he talks.

In a second, I make a decision. I need to get away. I run to the left, dodging his outstretched arms, and make my way towards the pool. If I can get to the other side of it, then I'll be safe. I can't explain my logic, even to myself, but it seems like a solid plan.

He follows suit, and he's faster than I expected. His hand grasps the back of my top and he pulls me to a stop. Finally, I'm able to scream but just as the sound leaves my lungs, his palm is pressed across my mouth.

"Be quiet. We need to be quiet. They can't know what we know. They. I don't know, they… They were everywhere. They know it all. Lucas. Lucas knew it all. Lucas knew I was a bad man. A very bad man." He says, emotion beginning to take him over. I use the lapse in his concentration to shove him away from me. He stumbles backwards, through the open door of the cabin next to the pool.

Before he can stand, I pull the door to a close and using a nearby pole, the kind used to clean debris from pools, I manage to prevent him from turning the handle and opening the door.

I watch as the handle jiggles and he pounds on the door, dreading the moment he breaks free. Eventually, the movement stops and I can hear him whimpering from the other side. I need to get help. Michael has snapped under the weight of his guilt and I need somebody to help me deal with him.

With a sprint, I run back towards the bar. Back to Robert and safety in numbers.

Chapter Fifteen

I needn't have run so fast - by the time I reach the bar, there's a congregation awaiting me. My muffled scream had done its job and caught the attention of my fellow holiday-makers.

Stephen is standing with Penny in the bar, their necks craning as they try to get a good look around the resort. Robert appeared looking ruffled and red in the face. The reason for this is soon revealed as Sam appears just behind him. Only Robert Castro could find his libido the day after seeing a dead body.

My feet slow as a sense of safety descends upon me. These people will help me. They'll restrain Michael until the police get here. Then I can at least stop worrying about every shadow, knowing that the perpetrator is taken care of. He all but admitted to killing Lucas during his ramblings, if nothing else, he at least gave away his motive. And it was exactly as I thought. He killed Lucas because he knew Michael was a bad man. That's what Michael had told me after all. That he was a bad man.

"Help," I gasp, despite knowing my words won't make it to them. The adrenaline that had driven me in this direction, away from Michael and his threats, was fading. Shock was setting in. My mind ripped like a spilt bag of rice. Pieces, words, memories scattering around me. No longer making sense when seen from a distance. Despite the heat of the rising sun, I feel cold. So very cold.

It feels as though the world exists on the other side of a window and I'm just observing. Watching with interest as Robert, Penny and Stephen move towards me. Sam rolls her eyes in the background and continues to stand by the bar. Busying herself by tidying up the glassware we'd left behind. Four glasses now, not three. She must have joined Robert for a drink before they disappeared together for some fun.

Will Stephen have noticed? Will she be in trouble? I hope not. The girl might not like me but I knew how persuasive Robert could be, and she must be feeling some level of shock at what had happened to Lucas. We all were in some form or another. For all I know she'd been a fan of his. She seemed around the right age for it.

Robert is standing in front of me now, his hand passing through the barrier around me. It feels sluggish on my shoulder. Penny steps through the glass surrounding the world and places her hand on my other shoulder. Between the two, I can feel them supporting my body weight. At least I assume they are. I know I'm not anymore. My feet want to move. They're desperate to move, but I've lost the ability to tell them to do so. I'm stuck in this moment as a chill takes over my blood.

I need to pull myself together. I have to lead them to Michael before he breaks out. What if he escapes and finds Fiona? She's still out in the resort. Alone.

"Emma? Emma, are you okay?" Robert asks, placing his hands gently on my face. I've dreamt of staring into his eyes so many times, but not like this. Never like this.

"Fiona." I sigh. Robert's face falls in sadness. He thinks something bad has happened. "We have to warn her." He recovers his composure and nods at me, speaking words I can't quite hear. It's like his mouth is working slower than his vocal chords.

"Michael. You have to help me. Michael is a bad man. Bad man." I need to keep talking. Talking will help me push back against the shock, because that's what's happening to me. I'm going into shock. I've watched enough medical dramas to recognise the symptoms.

Dad used to joke that I was the family's GP when another one of my home diagnoses matched their actual doctor's decision. Maybe I should have gone into medicine. No, that wouldn't have made any sense for me. I don't like blood. Don't like death.

I remember her body hanging in the living room. A bottle of wine dropped to the floor. A dinner date I should never have delayed. Her legs swinging in a non-existent breeze.

Dad's heart attack when I was twenty-two. Christmas dinner smeared across the carpet as we performed first aid under the guidance of the emergency services operator. The paramedics treading sprouts out of the front door as they wheeled him to the ambulance. Mum never cooked sprouts again, didn't matter really, none of us ate them.

Lucas. Lucas dying in an impossible situation. The empty floor around him. No chair. There was no chair.

Michaels's confession. His threat. His skin upon mine. The look of fear in his eyes.

"What happened?" Stephen's voice is firm, and it's the first thing to break through the fog that had descended upon me the moment I'd realised I was safe.

"Michael killed Lucas." I say, sure of his guilt based on the interaction we'd just had. He may not have said as much but perhaps when they'd medicated him out of whatever frenzy he was in, he'd be able to give some answers. Give closure to Lucas's family and friends.

Penny's hand falls from my shoulder, but Roberts's remains firm. He looks around us, assessing the area for danger. No longer questioning my paranoia.

"Where is he?" he asks, a protective growl in his voice I'd heard often on screen.

"I locked him in a cabin." I nearly laugh at my reply. It seems so ludicrous for me, Emma, to have locked a murderer in a cabin using a pool cleaning rod. It had happened though. I could still feel the shadow of the metal bar in the grip of my hand as I shoved it under the handle.

"Show us," demands Stephen and I oblige, wordlessly leading them toward the pool.

The first thing I notice as the pathway winds towards it is the open cabin door. The pole is lying discarded in the bushes nearby. He's escaped. Terror replaces shock and I grip onto Robert's arm, wanting to pull him back from the path we've set ourselves on. Michael could hide anywhere right now, ready to pounce. Ready to take his revenge on me for discovering the truth and locking him away.

The second thing I notice as we round the corner and see the pool is how beautifully the tails of

Michael's jacket look as they float in the water. They're moving in unison with him, like beautiful grey wings. I watch them peacefully enjoying themselves until suddenly they are thrashing around, disturbed from their relaxing float in the sun by Robert and Stephen diving into the pool.

They pull Michael from the water and throw him onto his back. His face is colourless and his eyes are wide open, staring up at the sun. You really shouldn't stare directly at the sun, it's so bad for your eyesight.

Robert is shouting at Michael, with all manner of expletives, explaining how he doesn't get to die. He doesn't get to escape like this. I watch him and it's almost like I'm sitting in a cinema at thirteen, watching him play the hero in some long-forgotten blockbuster.

Fiona suddenly enters the screen, stage right. Standing just behind Robert as he beats on Michael's chest, hand covering her mouth in shock. Penny's just beside me and I can hear Sam's footsteps following us up the path. She kept her distance, wanting to seem aloof and uninterested, but nobody could ignore the frustration in Robert's cries. The screen is descending around the world once again. I'm trapped behind it, unable to process anything.

Robert leans back from Michael, soaked to the bone and exhausted. He shakes his head at Stephen and the two of them stare down at Michael's body. Because that's what he is now. A body. A body that escaped justice.

Stephen leans forward and straightens Michael's jacket in an attempt at respect. As he does so, something catches his attention. He reaches inside the lapel and pulls out a plastic bag. Even from here, I can see the white powder. Drugs.

"This weekend is cursed," mutters Penny, her voice cutting through the numbness around me.

Drugs? There were drugs in Michael's jacket? I mean, that would explain a lot. It would explain why he was behaving in such a manic way. It would explain how he came to drown in the pool.

"What a terrible accident." sighs Sam.

Yes. Drugs would explain a lot of things. Except for two things running through my mind.

Michael was staunchly anti-drugs. His parents had been killed by a strung-out driver when he was twenty-two, and since then he'd campaigned tirelessly to make the streets cleaner of addiction. It's one of the few things he ever spoke about that I believed in.

There's never been even a whiff of a scandal about him regarding drugs. In fact, when it was found that drugs were being consumed in the House of Commons, he was front and centre of the debate calling for those caught to lose their jobs- even some prominent members of his own party. He had no sympathy or loyalty at that moment, he just wanted the guilty parties punished.

No, drugs and Michael don't make sense. The only way it would make sense would be if he were the finest actor the world had ever seen, and I've watched enough of his debates where he's covering a lie to know that isn't the case.

The second thing that drugs couldn't explain was Michael's jacket. He wasn't wearing one when I locked him in the cabin. The temperature was already balmy and he would have had no need for it. Besides, a grey suit jacket would have looked ridiculous with his chino shorts and bright shirt. I would have noticed the fashion faux-pau. The only answer would be if he had escaped, made his way back to his villa, and had chosen a formal jacket to wear back to the pool for a little drug-fuelled swim No. It didn't make any sense.

My eyes flick over to the pole thrown to the side in the bushes. There isn't a dent or a bend to be seen. It's as pristine as when I used it to lock Michael in the cabin. If he had broken out, he would have had to snap the pole. It should be underneath the open door, at least in half. Instead, it's been thrown off to the left, far away from the door.

Michael didn't do drugs. He wasn't wearing a jacket. He couldn't have broken free. It was all a series of impossibilities. The only explanation for the scene before me was that it was staged.

Someone here had killed Michael.

Someone standing around this pool right now.

Chapter Sixteen

Perhaps I should take up poker when I make it home, because somehow, despite the realisation that someone around me was a killer, I remain calm. At least outwardly. Inside my chest, my heart is beating so hard I'm sure it's trying to escape, but my face gives nothing away.

"Stephen?" I ask as I approach him, keeping my eyes diverted from Michael's body. "Stephen? Do we have an update on the police?" I keep my voice calm and neutral, not wanting anyone to hear the shrill fear behind my words. With two deaths in as many days, the presence of law enforcement was more important than ever.

"No. No. They haven't relayed any updates yet. The water is still too choppy for them to travel." He dusts off his knees as he stands regarding Michael for a moment. Bag of powder still in his hand, he looks down at it sadly. "It ruins so many lives." I nod in agreement, the only way to keep up the pretence that I believe in this charade. For all I know, the killer is watching me at this moment, waiting to pick out their next victim. Maybe Michael got too close to the truth, or Lucas discovered what was about to happen. Who knows? Either way, they were both dead.

"Michael had blood on his trousers." I remember out loud. "Not a lot, but it was there when he attacked me." It's hard to say the word attack now that I have doubts. What if somebody had laced his food with something that had caused him to act like that?

Something, or someone, had done something to him to cause that reaction. His pupils had been dilated, his movements jerky and his speech slurred. How had I not put the pieces together in the moment?

Simple really. I was too afraid to focus on logic when faced with what I perceived to be a danger. So certain my fate was about to be sealed that I didn't stop to see the full picture. Michael had been drugged. Somebody had needed him to lose his mind. To enable them to set up his death to look like a drug-induced accident. I might have bought into the story too if I hadn't known so much about his political stances.

The sky seems clear of any clouds or bad weather, but I guess it might be a different story on the other side of the complex's walls. Stephen had no reason to lie about the police. Every death was a mark against Hotel Horizen's reputation. If this weekend was marred any further, then Stephen wouldn't be able to list this weekend on his CV for future employers. It would be too horrific to include. He'd have to rehash the memories at every job interview with an intrigued employer.

"Perhaps we should go look in his room?" offers Fiona, now standing at my side. Her fingers brush against mine and I want to take her hand, but our kiss seems so long ago now that I don't want to be assumed presumptuous. As though she could read my mind, I feel the heat of her palm in mine.

"Well, I, for one, am getting the hell out of here," announces Penny. "Something's not right and I'm not sticking around to find out what." She's the sanest of all of us, and she's right. We need to find a way to leave rather than wait like sitting ducks until the police can arrive.

"If the water is too dangerous for the police to travel across, what makes you think you'll be able to?" asks Robert. His tone isn't unkind but his words are. He's exasperated.

"I'd rather be stuck out on the water than spend another hour here." She turns to leave and then seems to remember something. "My phone. I'd like my mobile back." she orders Sam.

"I'll have to get the key," obliges Sam.

"Do it then," Penny replies sharply and she watches with a scowl as Sam hurries off. "I suggest you all pack your bags too. Stephen, where's the staff boat?"

"Staff boat?"

"The one that you used to get here. Surely there's at least a paddle boat on this blasted island?"

He thinks for a moment and slowly nods.

"There might be a maintenance one we could use. It's not the most reliable though."

"If it floats, it will suffice. We'll leave a message for the police at reception when we leave and if we're stranded out there, then they will find us."

"You realise the ocean is a pretty big place?" asks Fiona, a touch of sarcasm laced between her words.

"Yes Fiona. I'm also aware that it's wet. What you may not be aware of, however, is that something isn't right with this island. Maybe it's cursed, haunted, god I don't know. But something isn't right and we need to leave now."

I find it strange that Penny has leapt to the island being haunted before she considers the possibility of foul play amongst its inhabitants. I guess, even now, she believes in the good of people.

"Pack and meet me at my villa. If you aren't there in twenty minutes, I will leave without you. Stephen, meet me at the check-in desk in half an hour and we'll all board the boat together." She's so commanding that it's comforting.

Finally, somebody is in charge and has a plan. I watch as she walks off towards her villa, shoulders pulled up high, confidence being left behind in every footstep and I long to be perfect Penny in that moment. Imagine being so sure of the world that you can take hold of a nightmare and simply tell it 'no.'

Not wanting to disobey direct orders, and finding having a clear directive is quelling my worries, I do as I'm told and walk towards my villa with every intention of packing my bag. Just as I turn the path towards my front door, a voice calls out my name. I have a mental flashback to just an hour ago when Michael did the same from the bushes. He'd asked for my help. I should have listened. The man may have morally been a monster but he didn't deserve to be killed like that.

"Emma," comes the voice again. It's not Michael, not a ghost of guilt here to haunt me. It was Fiona. She steps towards me, tears in her eyes, and wraps her arms around me. The closeness of her, the warmth from her skin, lessens the shock that was still lingering within me. "Ohh Emma." She sighs into my neck and I'm ashamed to say I feel a shudder of attraction. I wasn't going to be like Robert. Two people have died. It is not the time for a holiday romance. No matter how delectable she smelt.

"We need to pack," I say. Using every ounce of self-control to gently peel myself from her grip.

"Can we do it together? Yours first, then mine?"

She doesn't want to be alone. I didn't ask anyone to accompany me to pack because I didn't want to seem like a baby. Nobody else seemed fearful of their own company. I was grateful she'd followed me, that she felt the same fear as I did.

"Ten minutes here. Ten minutes at yours?" I offer and she nods gratefully.

Truth be told, there isn't much I'm desperate to take with me. Most of my possessions are easily replaceable. There are only two things I want to pack - my notebook and my camera. I need the photos of Lucas's room for posterity, a way to add weight to my theory about what happened to him. I just had to hope that the investigators found the idea of Michael taking drugs as outlandish and suspicious as I did, as there was no way to sneak back and take a photograph of him now.

I couldn't let these crimes be swept under the carpet, no matter what the men had done in their personal lives.

Michael had been greedy and that greed had cost innocent people to lose their lives. It was a horrific crime but one he deserved to answer to in a court of law. If Robert were to be believed, Lucas had more than a passing interest in girls at the older end of the illegal status, a groomer more than a paedophile. He deserved to answer for his actions in the court of public opinion. In truth, death was an easy way out for both of them.

I open my door and step inside. Fiona follows

suit. I had hoped to bring her back here under different circumstances but that was twenty-four hours ago, back when everyone was alive and drinking happily together. We should all be lounging around the pools right now, waiting to be called in for another gourmet dinner, already sad that we'd be leaving in two more nights.

Picking up the beach bag I'd thankfully packed, I move around my room with speed, shoving a few items of clothing, my notebook, sun cream, and the paperback Fiona lent me on the flight inside. Noticing this, she gives me a sad little smile.

"This is not how I imagined our weekend ending. Becoming castaways on a boat that might not even float."

"What did you imagine?" I ask, wanting to know what she'd had planned for me in the moments before I'd spotted Lucas's body. I know we don't have time to play pretend but I can't resist. She raises an eyebrow in my direction.

"Oh. I imagined quite a bit. Could barely keep my mind focused when I was getting ready for dinner. Kept thinking about your legs, your lips, your..." Her eyes drop to my breasts, letting her sentence hang in the air around us. All I want is to go to her. To throw her onto my bed, climb on top of her, and place my lips on every hidden part of her. Sweat beads at the top of my lips as I imagine the sounds of her panting my name as I finally, finally give into her pleas and take her.

Without quite meaning to, I glance at the ticking clock behind her head. We have six minutes left to finish packing and head to her villa. Fourteen minutes until we needed to be at Penny's place, ready to escape.

At this moment, I have a new understanding of Robert's libido. I may have judged him too harshly for fooling around with Sam just hours after we cut down Lucas's body. Something about knowing death was all around us made the idea of an orgasm that much more enticing.

Six minutes. Six minutes wasn't long. But it could be enough.

I take Fiona's hands and lead her to my bed. Her eyes are large with want and I know she has the same desperate urge to feel alive that I do. Much more gently than I want to, I push her onto my bed. Her head hits my pillow and I throw my legs across her stomach, straddling her, looking down at her beautiful face. A face I was going to contort with pleasure before these six minutes were up. Five minutes now.

With slow and precise movements I open the buttons of her blouse. She sighs with relief as I finally unhook the last one. The bra she's wearing is functional but a cup size too small. The top of her breasts are hanging out haphazardly, exposing the very beginnings of her nipple. Leaning down slowly, I nuzzle the cup from the right-hand side, peeling it off of her with gentle teeth. My breath on her nipple causes it to tighten, an exclamation of relief escapes from her and I feel her hips struggle to move. Squeezing my thighs together, I hold her in place.

Just as I'm about to spell the alphabet on her exposed breast, she slides her hands up under the pillow. Shit. Shit. The camera. The fucking camera is under my pillow.

Her hand fiddles around with it, as though she's trying to work out what it is just by touch. It's one of those retro rectangular ones though, difficult to distinguish, and if I remember correctly, I'd slid the cover over the lens. Hopefully, she gives up and wants to stay in the moment with me. Three minutes. We only have three minutes.

I'm frozen in time, my lips just above her breast as I keep a watchful eye on her. She's noticed the slackening of my grip around her waist, the fact I've stopped teasing her. She opens her eyes that had just fluttered closed in expectant ecstasy.

"Emma?" she asks, worried about me. I can't reply. Slowly, painfully slowly, she pulls the camera out from under the pillow and regards it.

This time, when she pushes her hips up towards me, I let her. I swing my legs over and sit on the bed next to her.

She's playing with the lens cover, flicking it open and closed. Open and closed. Her features are hyper-fixated on what she's found. I can't read her expression but I can tell by the fact she hasn't spoken that the moment has passed.

She looks up at the clock. Two minutes left.

"I think I'd better go pack." She says, placing the camera down on the mattress between us. Silently she buttons her shirt back up and stands.

"I'll come with you," I offer.

"No. No, I think it's best if I meet you at Penny's."

"It's not what you think." I protest. Needing her to give me this last minute to explain to her.

"I think you smuggled a camera into the resort. I think you probably intended to publish any photos you took with it. I think you couldn't respect the promise of privacy on this island. Most of all though, I think you misled me."

"I would never take photos of you. Of any of you!" She needs to understand that I just wanted to take photos of the resort.

"Yes, but it's easy to say that now, isn't it? I only have your word for it."

She's at my front door now, turned away from me. I stand from the bed and move towards her. Our last minute is up.

"I'll see you at Penny's." she says as she walks out of the door. I listen to her footsteps echo down the stairs as she leaves.

We only had ten minutes. How could everything go so wrong in just ten minutes?

Chapter Seventeen

I drag my feet across the path as I head toward Penny's villa, cursing myself for being such an idiot. I should have never brought a camera with me. Or, at the very least, I should have just left it in my suitcase. Fiona wouldn't give me a chance to explain myself, and she's going to mistrust me even further when she finds out who I really am.

Once the police get here, my fabricated backstory will be shot to shit. The fact I'm a penniless nobody will add even more weight to her suspicion that I was going to sell private photos of them all to the press. I mean, she wasn't completely off the mark. I was, am, planning to write about this trip, but the only photos I would ever have included would have been of the resort. To show that I wasn't telling tales about its decadence.

She'll never believe that though. I've blown a chance at a genuine connection because of the part I insisted on playing. I should have told her the truth when we were sitting by the pool alone. Should have told her before we kissed. And I definitely should have told her before I took her onto my bed. No wonder she's annoyed. I'd be steaming if somebody had done all of that to me. I should have just settled for a quick fumble with Robert. There's no doubt that's all it would have been to him, no pesky feelings allowing guilt to get in the way of passion.

As my mind drifts towards the 'could have beens' of the weekend, I spot Sam and Stephen walking just ahead of me. At least somebody had some fun this weekend, I think to myself as I scowl at Sam's back. Which was unkind. Other than being cold towards me, she's done nothing wrong. I'm just jealous that she found a release for the pent-up energy and nerves I know we're all feeling.

My friends used to joke that funerals made them horny. I never really understood the link between death and lust until Fiona walked into my bedroom. Knowing how short and precious life could be just ramped up every nerve in me.

Sam and Stephen pause outside Penny's door, exchanging words that don't reach my ears, before Stephen reaches out and gives a firm knock. I'm just at the start of the entrance path when Penny opens the door.

"Emma, where's Fiona?" she calls out. Ignoring the staff members in front of her. "I thought she went with you?"

There's a touch of concern in her voice and I understand. If something wasn't right on this island, now was the time to stick together.

Understanding the panic in her voice, her need for us all to stick to our plans, lessened the shock when she opened her villa door wider and Robert was standing just behind her. On Friday morning she could barely stand being on the same aeroplane as him and now, here she was, nearly forty-eight hours later, standing on the threshold of her villa with him. Fear is remarkable at quietening hate.

"She decided to go pack and meet me here." I offer, trying to keep the disappointment from my face. Robert notices though and shoots me a sympathetic look. He knows what it's like to be on the receiving end of Fiona's temper. Maybe we'll find a moment together to swap battle stories before she arrives.

"May we come inside?" asks Stephen, fed up with being ignored.

"Did you bring our phones?" asks Penny, directing her attention to Sam. Her face clouds as the woman shakes her head in response.

"It appears the key to the safe is missing," explains Stephen. Penny sighs in exasperation.

"Did you at least find the boat, or is that missing, too?" She believes the two of them are incompetent and is making no attempt to mask this.

"Ah. No. We found the boat but…"

"Someone's destroyed it!" interrupts Sam, her face pale. She looks towards Robert, hoping for some level of familiarity to comfort her but she receives nothing. I feel for her.

"What do you mean?" asks Robert, addressing his question to Stephen as though he completed his sentence. As though Sam had never spoken. Poor girl.

"The hull appears to have been broken in several places. Damage that could have occurred naturally in the seasonal storms. We rarely use the boat, you see." Stephen shoots daggers at Sam. "There's no need for alarm. I'm sure it has been in that state for a while now."

By now I'm standing at the front door, beach bag over my arm, unsure of what the plan would be.

"Still. We'd be better off waiting by the jetty for the police to arrive," Penny says, trying to rationalise the situation as it unfurls around us.

"Are you sure? Maybe it's a better idea to stay here," urges Robert. "At least here we know what we're up against."

"Do we? Do we really, Robert?" she asks.

"Emma, what do you think we should do?" he asks me, drawing me into a decision I want no part in making.

"Yes. Emma. Why don't you tell us all what to do?" Fiona's voice simmers with resentment as she walks past me and straight through the front door, Robert and Penny move out of her path just in time, narrowly avoiding a shoulder barge.

"I have a suggestion, if I may?" offers Stephen as I watch as Robert excuses himself from the conversation and follows Fiona inside.

My heart catches in my throat. In a matter of minutes, I'll lose the only other ally I have on this island. Fiona will confide in Robert about the camera and he will have the same reaction as her. He will also think of me as nothing more than an opportunist.

"Go on," orders Penny. If there had ever been any doubt that she was our Most Valuable Player, it was gone now.

"I've spoken to the staff and they've all agreed to act as security for each of you, for the rest of the weekend, or until the police arrive, whichever happens sooner."

Penny throws her hands up, turns on her heel, and walks inside the villa. Without hesitation, Stephen follows her footsteps, then Sam, and finally me. I pull the door closed behind me. We don't live in a barn after all. I watch as Penny paces up and down the hallway, biting back words that even she knows are too harsh. Over in the kitchen, I can see Fiona and Robert talking quietly. Their heads hung low towards each other.

Finally, Penny speaks, but her voice is low and deep, a warning to Stephen that she's at the edge of her patience. "I don't think you truly understand the issue here, Stephen. We don't want security. We want to leave. We need to leave. Something on this island isn't right and that wouldn't change even if I had twenty personal security guards."

Sam takes a step away from Stephen, perhaps wanting to distance herself from Penny's frustration. She peers out of the window by the front door, taking the occasional glance behind her towards the kitchen where Robert and Fiona are still sitting locked in conversation. For a brief moment, Fiona looks up at me. Our eyes lock and I take a step towards the kitchen to talk to her. Then, just as quickly, she looks away, irritated by my presence. Robert quickly shoots me a sympathetic smile over her shoulder. He, at least, has been on the receiving end of her temper before. There's hope that I might not lose all my allies here.

"I promise you I understand the severity of the situation. Two deaths in such close succession is something I've never experienced in my career. But you have to believe me, Mrs. Atwell, nothing is going on beyond a case of depression and an accident. There is no monster we need to run from. Our best and safest course of action is to stay put. Put your faith in me, I implore you."

Rather than responding verbally, Penny huffs and walks away from Stephen, who stands awkwardly in the hallway. Before he has a chance to lock eyes with me and form an alliance, I step across to where Sam stands. joining her in staring mindlessly out of the window.

"You don't belong here," she hisses at me quietly and I'm taken aback by her words. Even now she dislikes me. Even when we're facing a crisis.

"And yet here I am," I reply, channelling Rebecca's tone as I do so. Working with my boss for as long as I have seemed to have granted me some personality perks. Sam needs to know she can't belittle me, not right now. Not with Fiona just feet away. I have to be the one to tell her the truth, to explain how I came to be here this weekend. I can't let Sam's spite destroy what could be the last chance I have of making amends.

"You shouldn't be here," she says, ignoring my response. Her eyes are fixed with precision on the path in front of the door, as though she can't even bring herself to look at me. I decide to be petty and follow suit, turning my attention away from her and towards the outside world. If she wants to freeze me out, then I can do the same.

A young man who couldn't be older than twenty-three, comes into view. Dressed in baggy white trousers and a side-buttoned chef's coat - kitchen staff. This must be the security that Stephen was referring to. I take in the stranger's profile, and I don't mean this unkindly, but he hardly looked as though he'd be a match for a spider, let alone somebody trying to harm us. Still, if there are more staff members on their way, then numbers will at least be on our side.

In reality this situation doesn't make sense. If somebody on the island wanted to kill us, then they could have just put poison into our first meal and been done with it. But to go to the trouble of staging Lucas's murder as a suicide and Michael's as an accident tells me a different story, a scarier one. Whoever's behind this doesn't just want to kill us. They want to torture us mentally. Make us fear them. Break us with terror until we can't take anymore.

That's far darker than your run-of-the-mill murderer on countless podcasts about true crimes. Some people kill because they had the opportunity to, or because they felt they had to, and some people kill because they like it. That's who we're dealing with here. A true-blue psychopath.

I'm drawn from my own thoughts by a shout from Stephen. It had sounded like he told everyone to 'get down' but that wouldn't make any sense in our current situation. I catch sight of something outside the window before a hand firmly pushes me to the floor. Looking around me, I notice that Stephen, Penny, and Robert are all lying down on the floorboards, hands covering their faces.

I turn my head to the side and am surprised to find Fiona there. She's the one who pushed me down, and now she's lying next to me, one arm thrown across the small of my back protectively as she stares straight ahead under the crack at the bottom of the door.

The only sound in the villa is Sam's piercing screams that come almost in a pattern. Between each yell, she cries, and no matter how many people hiss at her to be silent, she doesn't pay attention, her knees drawn into her chest as she rocks with terror.

"Is the door locked?" whispers Robert between the noises being emitted by Sam. Fiona raises her head slightly, then shakes it.

"Lock the doors!" Stephen orders as he shuffles along the floor in an army crawl. Fiona follows suit, sliding her body along until she's underneath the door. Then she slowly pulls herself up onto her knees and in one jerky movement closes the lock on the door.

"What's going on?" I ask, keeping my voice low and directing my question to Fiona.

"Didn't you hear the shot?" she asks, confusion on her face. Shot? I can't remember hearing anything before Stephen told us to lie down. I had been standing by the window next to Sam, looking at the young man sent to protect us, and then…

And then…

Then the young man had fallen to the floor. My ears were ringing. His handsome face splayed in pieces on either side of him as he lay crumpled on the ground. Sam had drawn in a breath and the screaming had begun.

"Oh god," I say and my hand shakes. I press it down into the floorboard to control it. Hoping to push my fear out of my body and into the ground. Oh god, I am going to vomit.

"This is not how it's supposed to end," mutters Penny over and over to herself. Between that and Sam's screaming, we have a symphony of noise around us that's making it hard to think straight.

"For Christ's sake, Stephen, will you shut her up?" spits Robert as Stephen returns to the hallway after locking the back door.

"Sam. Sam. Pull yourself together," Stephen begs as he crawls over towards her. Her expression is blank. She's no longer in the room with us.

"Get her out of here!" Demands Robert.

"I'll take care of it," offers Penny out of nowhere. She's finally stopped chanting her mantra and stands.

"Stay away from the windows!" warns Robert and Penny obeys, ducking out of the line of sight.

She leans in close to Sam and whispers something. Whatever it is, it has the desired effect and the screaming finally stops. Penny always had a way with people. Sobs are still echoing from Sam's mouth but without the constant harping, it's already easier to breathe.

Penny, still careful to avoid the windows, leads Sam up the stairs.

"Close the curtains up there!" directs Fiona, then she moves around the room, pulling them closed around us. Robert copies her movements on the opposite side of the house until we're left with our own shadows.

I need to be useful so I drag a coffee table from the living room and move it towards the front door. Stephen helps me lift it into place and we push it up against the front door handle. Barricading it closed in the same way I had done to Michael. The juxtaposition isn't lost on me.

When we're all sure we've done the best we can to protect ourselves, we stand in the middle of the living room, panting lightly at the exertio n and the fear. Penny comes back down the stairs.

"I've put Sam to bed."

"So, what's the situation here?" asks Robert, looking at Stephen for an answer.

"I...I don't know," he stutters.

"You can't deny it anymore. Something's wrong

on this island," says Penny.

"Something is more than wrong, someone is out there," Fiona points to the front door, "trying to kill us."

"You don't know that we're the targets," protests Robert.

"Who else is it bloody going to be? Think about it. It's exactly like we said. Lucas. Michael. All along we told you that something was going on!" Fiona is frustrated and airing her grievances. As much as I agree with every word, now isn't the time.

"If they have a master key, can they get in?" I ask.

"No. There are very few suites that actually have a key for entry on the island. A security feature our architect dreamed up. Means that no one can access the guests when they require privacy," answers Stephen. It at least meant nobody could sneak a peek at their favourite celebrity whilst they were getting changed. And at least in these circumstances, it meant so long as we protected the doors, nobody could get in.

We all stand in a circle, looking at each other. Waiting for someone to speak, for someone to come up with a plan to get us out of this danger and off of this island. There's only so long we can stay barricaded in this villa.

Right now we're easy pickings. The windows could easily be shattered by bullets, or a fire could be started, or they could simply storm the doors. There were all manner of ways to kill us whilst we were standing around trying to keep ourselves safe.

Not to mention we have around forty-eight hours until the speedboats arrive back to collect us for our flight. We have no food, no way to contact the outside world, and right now, no plan. This was not the holiday I'd imagined.

Chapter Eighteen

"Isn't there a spare key for the safe?" asks Robert, referring to the safe that holds our phones and perhaps our only chance of escape.

"No. It wouldn't be very secure to have keys lying around the place, now would it? Not when personal phones can hold such a wealth of information," replies Stephen, a glint in his eye at the second half of his sentence. The way he flits between personalities makes me uneasy. He had done it when we first arrived and my opinion of it hadn't changed since. Either he was exceptionally good at shutting off any empathy for the benefit of his professionalism, or he was a real-life Jekyll and Hyde. Two completely opposite personalities sharing one body.

"Well, what about staff members' phones?" asks Penny, an idea formulating in her mind.

"Kept in the safe as well. For guest's privacy. Although..."

"Although what?" presses Penny.

"Although Sam often got reprimanded for sneaking hers on site with her. She'd never spread gossip though...not Sam." As though any of us care right now whether she was snapping unflattering bikini photos of us.

"I'll go ask her!" responds Fiona, taking the stairs two at a time, hope of rescue providing a spring in her step.

"Do you think it's terrorists?" I ask. It's the only logical reason for somebody to be on the island hunting us. The terrorist group who managed to take out this many VIPs in one swoop would be one to take seriously. World leaders wouldn't be able to ignore their actions.

"I don't know," replies Robert with a sad shrug. He looks at me apologetically, wishing he had the answers.

We stand uneasily in our circle and wait for her to return. When she does, her feet are soft on the stairs and her face is pale. She looks as though now she might vomit and I can't help my instinct as I move towards her. Robert beats me to it though, and takes her by the arm down the last two steps, steadying her shaking movements.
"She's dead," says Fiona, glancing back up the stairs. "Sam is…she's dead."

I inhale sharply, turning my attention to Stephen to offer him comfort. He and Sam had seemed close. Noticing the look in my eyes, he takes a step back and raises both his hands. No. He doesn't want my apologies or condolences for his loss. He wants to maintain his composure, at least for now.

Turning away from us, he walks into the kitchen and we listen as he opens and closes cupboards until he finds what he's looking for. The tap runs. He fills his glass and takes long deep gulps of the liquid. There's a pause in his movement and I imagine he's using it to centre himself. To take in the news about his colleague.

After finding Fiona somewhere to sit, Robert takes his turn climbing the staircase, wanting to see the situation for himself. Despite the bile in my throat, I move to follow him. Penny grabs my arm tightly and holds me in place.

"Don't."

I briefly try to jostle my arm free from her grasp but it's no use. She doesn't loosen the pressure until I move backward, away from the step. I look at her in irritation and she softly shakes her head.

"Why?" I ask.

"You've seen enough for one weekend," she replies. And she isn't wrong. Lucas, Michael, the young man, and now Sam. Bodies were piling up all around us and I'd had the misfortune of witnessing three of them. "Besides, somebody needs you." She looks over at Fiona as she speaks, who's sitting on a sofa with her head in her hands. I nod and move towards her.

"Can I sit?" I ask. Fiona nods her head and slowly I take the seat next to her. Without looking at me, she reaches out to grab one of my hands and grips it tightly, trying to draw strength from me.

"Upstairs is secure," announces Robert as he comes back down the stairs, nausea painted across his features. Whatever state Sam is in, it isn't pleasant.

"How could this happen?" asks Stephen, rejoining the group.

"I don't know, but I'm certain we would have heard somebody break in upstairs," replies Robert.

"That must mean..." Penny let her sentence hang around us and then it hits me. She thinks somebody in this room killed Sam. That one of us is the killer.

The only problem with that is it leaves two suspects, her and Fiona. Nobody else has gone upstairs, aside from Robert just now. Why would Penny make an observation that would put herself under the spotlight?

"You aren't suggesting...?" asks Stephen, not

finishing his question, instead turning to stare at Fiona with concern. I watch him measure her up with his eyes, weighing up whether she's capable of such violence.

"Of course she isn't suggesting that. Are you Penny?" I ask, squeezing Fiona's hand. I know she's innocent. If anything, this just cements my suspicions of Penny. She had time and motive to kill Lucas. She wasn't accounted for after we left the restaurant this morning either, before Michael was killed. There are too many coincidences. Inviting suspicion onto herself is a risky move if she is guilty though. Risky, but clever.

Penny looks at Fiona, who is still staring at the floor in shock. "All I know is she was alive when I put her to bed," she replies.

"And we just take your word for that, do we?" I say, unable to help the anger in my words. How dare she stand there and accuse Fiona of something she is so clearly guilty of. I calculate the distance between myself and Penny, fantasising about striking her across her lying face.

"Enough!" shouts Robert, bringing our squabbling to a quick end. "Nobody here killed Sam. Not unless they showered and changed their outfit without any of us noticing."

We all look at him questioningly, not sure quite what he's getting at.

"Her throat was slit. The amount of blood...it would be impossible to do that to someone and stay clean," says Fiona, her voice monotone. She glares up at Penny. "But thanks for the vote of confidence."

"Somebody must have gotten in through a window," says Stephen.

"All the windows are closed," replies Robert.

Stephen moves to stand in front of Rober, and the tension between them flashes with aggression that threatens to spill over. "They are now," he says.

"What are you suggesting?" Robert asks.

"You could have closed them when you went up to check. It would have been easy enough."

"Why would I do that?"

"Who knows? I'm just saying it's a possibility."

By now the two of them are practically touching noses and I'm waiting for the first fist to fly.

"Stop. Stop!" shouts Penny, inserting herself between the two men. A hand on each chest as she physically parts them. "None of this is going to help us."

Stephen tries to push his way forward, attempting to get near enough to Robert to hurt him. "Unless we guess the culprit correctly!" he yells. Penny is stronger than she looks though. She spins round to face him, placing both hands on his chest, and pushes him away. It's remarkable how much she's changed when it comes to Robert. When we'd first arrived, I imagine she would have paid good money to the first person to punch him. But now, here she was, putting herself in harm's way to protect him.

"That's quite enough. Look, Stephen, I know Sam's death is a shock to you. I know the two of you were close but she's gone now, and if we aren't careful we could be next," says Fiona, standing from the sofa, nerves evaporating. The testosterone in the air has woken her from the shock of finding Sam.

"It's nearly nightfall. I suggest we camp out here, regroup and then move just before dawn," suggests Penny, directing her conversation towards Fiona.

Towards the only other level head in the room.

"Surely moving at night would make more sense?" asks Fiona.

"The dark would work to their advantage as much as it would ours. Besides, we all need to rest. We'll be no good to anyone if we're exhausted."

She's right of course. I hadn't realised how tired I was until she mentioned it. Adrenaline had masked the fact that I haven't slept properly since the night before the flight. I imagine Fiona and Robert felt the same. It had been impossible to get a good night's sleep after discovering Lucas and all that went along with it.

"So, what do we do in the morning?" asks Robert, his breathing back to a regular rate now.

"In the morning, we'll make our way to Guest Services. When we get there, we'll use the landline to call for help. If we're lucky, they will have gotten cocky and left the safe open," replies Fiona, and Penny nods at her in agreement. It's as though there's a psychic link between them, formulating the same plan for our survival.

"That's on the other side of the island though," interjects Stephen, and he's not wrong.

Penny's villa is in a mirror image placement to mine. Located all the way at the back right-hand corner of the complex. Hidden behind some trees, next to the false sea pool that leads to the restaurant. Everyone is quiet for a moment, contemplating this complication.

"We could swim across and then use the bar for cover." I suggest.

"We'd be totally exposed," argues Robert.

"It would take us five minutes to swim to the

other side, twenty minutes to walk there." I have to stick to my guns about this. I know in my gut it's the right answer.

He's right, of course, that it will leave us exposed, but no more exposed than making our way around the pathways on foot. Sure, if we took that route there would be the occasional bush to hide in but mostly it was open space. We could be picked off one by one and have nowhere to hide, exactly the same risk if they found us in the pool.

Still - five minutes of danger beats twenty minutes of danger in my mind. It's simple maths.

Everyone considers my suggestion and I stand with bated breath, waiting for them to agree. Or to argue against me. Either way, I knew I was going to swim for my safety. They could do as they liked.

"Once we're across the pool, I need to go to my villa," agrees Robert.

"That's a complete detour from the check-in desk," argues Fiona, and I'm sure she's right. I may not know where Robert's villa is located but I know there's no accommodation between the bar and the front desk.

"Look. I'll go on my own if I have to."

"No one is going anywhere on their own," warns Penny.

"Everyone needs an alibi," adds Stephen with a sneer.

"That's not what I meant! I meant we're safer together."

"I'll go with Robert," I offer. I trust him. The more I think about it, the less I suspect him. He had no motive to hurt Michael and Lucas, no reason to kill Sam - especially after they'd fooled around. I'm sure it wasn't the hangover of a teenage crush influencing my judgment – he was a good man. I could tell that from the handful of conversations we'd had.

"Me too," adds Fiona and she smiles at me. "We'll stick together." Our little clique, was brought back together again by the most awful circumstances.

"What's so important that we need to risk three lives to retrieve it?" asks Penny.

"My gun," answers Robert gravely. For a moment everyone is quiet and then all hell breaks loose.

"A gun?"

"You brought a gun?"

"How do we know it wasn't your gun being fired?"

"That's ridiculous."

"Of all the things you've done so far."

"You might have brought them the weapon they're using!"

So many voices all overlapping each other, it's hard to keep track of who's talking. I might have even thrown a few accusations myself. The idea that somebody would bring a gun, or a weapon on holiday with them is foreign to me.

Living in England, the only guns I've ever seen have been at the bigger airports and that was enough to strike fear into me. But Robert is a cliché apparently, a yank who can't live without his steel best friend for four days.

"You're all forgetting one thing," Robert shouts above us all. It seems we're long past trying to keep our voices down. "That gun could end up saving our lives."

That silences us.

He's right. Other than a few kitchen knives we have very little to defend ourselves with. Having even just one gun will help to even the playing field.

"Why didn't you bring it with you when you went back to pack?" asks Penny, and it's a fair question. If he was so keen to have it in his possession, then it made sense he would have retrieved it at the first available moment.

"I didn't go back to pack. I kept my eye on each of you just to be sure you were safe and then came straight here. You even commented that I was the first man you knew who'd arrived early." He stares at Penny, worried that she'd forgotten their interaction.

"Oh yes. I'd forgotten," she adds, but something doesn't feel right about the way in which she's conceded to him. I can't put my finger on it but it's as though she's going along with a story she can't quite remember reading. Has the stress begun to affect her memory?

"Look. I think we all need to take a breath and get some rest. We'll sleep in shifts if everyone agrees?" suggests Fiona, adding some calm to the storm that's just been unleashed. We're behaving like caged animals, lashing out at each other at every opportunity.

Everyone nods and we split up into groups. Robert and Penny will rest first whilst Stephen, Fiona , and I keep an eye on the situation around us. I agree to this plan straight away and offer to keep watch over the kitchen door for any movement. It will give me a chance to sit on my own, regroup my thoughts and fill in my notebook for today.

Just as I'm about to hunker down into my watch

spot in the kitchen, Penny approaches me. She holds something in her hands towards me before she speaks.

"We've had a discussion and you're the one everyone trusts the most."

I'm shocked at the compliment. Maybe it's because I'm an outsider, and I've never run in the same circles and, therefore, the same dramas as the rest of them. She thrusts a plastic carry case into my hands. Inside, I can see four passports. Ah. So it's not a case of them having the most trust in me. I'm the group's donkey, required to cart around vital cargo.

I nod at her in agreement. Secretly I'm grateful for this responsibility and bag. It means I can transport my camera and notebook safely with me across the pool. And I don't have to worry about prying eyes picking over them.

Chapter Nineteen

It's Sunday morning now.

That's the first thought that slips across my groggy mind as Robert gently rouses me from sleep. Sunday. Friday morning feels like an entire lifetime ago. I can remember the drive to the airport, the bubbles of nerves in my stomach at the idea of the flight, and the panic I had about the boat ride. I almost want to laugh at that Emma.

The one before, as I've come to think of her. Sweet, naïve Emma who thought a boat ride or the company of celebrities was going to be the most nerve-racking part of the weekend. The Emma before me had been so beautifully clueless as to what lay before her. She had no idea that just forty-eight hours into the future everything would be upside down. That she'd be a completely different person, one fighting for her life. Just thirty-six hours left to make sure I stay alive and then salvation will be here.

Thirty-six hours until the speed boats are due to pick us up for our flight. That's all. Not a long time when you consider it. Easily an amount of time we could spend safely barricaded inside this villa.

I'm rethinking our idea of running for safety. Overnight, there have been no signs of anyone trying to enter or attack the villa. I'd started to believe we were safe here but then I took a look out of the window.

When I first peer out, just beyond the pool, I'm not sure what I'm seeing. A large mound of broken wooden furniture is smouldering in the distance. My breath catches in my throat and I try to stop myself from hyperventilating. They've built a pyre in the centre of the complex.

I pull my camera out of the plastic bag I'd moved it to last night, and lean out of the window, being careful not to make any sound. I don't know who's lurking around the perimeter after all. They might have just been keeping their heads down overnight to lull us into a false sense of security.

Using the zoom on my camera I try to make more sense of the smoke rising from the centre. Unfortunately, this particular bit of tech is about fifteen years old, and the zoom renders the photo blurry and unusable. Returning to its original frame rate, I snap a few photos of what I can see, then close the window and sit down just below it.

I scroll back through the images, wondering whether I should give the others the heads up about the fire when my finger freezes on the button.

There, on the screen, is a photo I definitely did not take. Or at least, one I definitely can't remember taking. It's Sam's body. In the room just over my head. Thick, dark, congealed blood that now looks brown surrounds her. Littering the walls of the room with violence, sprinkled across the bed in a halo around her. But what's most disturbing about the image, aside from the murder and the fact I didn't take it, is what's written on the wall above the bed Sam lies on. Penny. Stephen. Robert. Fiona. Emma.

Our five names were written in Sam's blood above her body. Had Fiona seen this when she went to check on Sam and found her dead? Is that why she was so shocked?

And why didn't Robert mention it after he'd checked the windows upstairs? Did they not feel it was important that we'd all been name-checked at a crime scene?

I'm feeling a range of emotions right now, from angry to terrified. The killer knew who we all were and they listed us off above their last victim. Was this the order we were due to die in? I don't want to die. Please don't let me die. I want to get home, get back to my job, see my parents, fall asleep in my shitty small bed, and spend all day working on spreadsheets people merely glance at and daydream about a better life. I just want to go back to that day in the office when Rebecca offered me her place on this trip. I want to say no thank you and push for a raise or a promotion instead. I just want to live. Please. Just let me live.

All my thoughts about cancelling our escape plan and staying put, of believing that we are safe in this villa, disappear when I look at that list of names. Robert reappears at my side and hands me a cup of black coffee.

"No milk, I'm afraid." He apologises.

I'm guessing all the fancy pods for the coffee machine have been used up whilst we were undertaking our sleep shifts. I don't blame the others. I had two cappuccinos myself whilst on shift. On autopilot, I reach for the coffee mug, forgetting that I'm still holding my camera.

Roberts's eyes glance at the screen.

"What the hell is that?" he asks in a low voice.

"I don't know. It was on the camera when I woke up."

"Those words. They weren't there last night. I would have noticed. I would have told you all."

"Are you sure?"

"Sure as anything. Fiona?" he calls her towards us and she obeys. "Do you remember any writing on the walls yesterday when you found Sam?"

She shudders at the memory.

"I don't know. I saw her lying there. All that blood and I just left. I had to get out of there." She pauses, catches her breath, brings herself back to the present. "Why?"

Robert lifts the camera from my hands and passes it to her. She gasps softly as she takes in the digital image in front of her. I watch as her eyes scan the list of names and her brows furrow.

"We need to leave. If you didn't see the words when you checked upstairs, then that means whoever killed Sam came back in the night. Or they never left." She glances towards the stairs, the one place none of us have dared venture since Robert returned from them yesterday. He'd said everything upstairs was secure but all he'd done was check the windows were locked. I'm sure he hadn't checked every nook and cranny. Anyone could be hiding up there.

"We need to leave. Now," she repeats, louder now, towards the hallway where Stephen and Penny are standing.

"I just need five minutes," protests Penny.

"Now," repeats Fiona, a flicker of charge in her eyes that warns the other woman not to argue against her. The power dynamic keeps switching between the two of them and I wonder who it's going to settle on when all of this ends. Because it has to end, doesn't it? This terror can't last forever. Thirty-six hours. I've just got to survive thirty-six hours.

We do as we're commanded and make our way to the back door. The men take charge, as they like to do, and lift the curtains slightly to peer outside, to check the coast is clear. It's not the most sensible decision, as anyone could be hiding, waiting to pounce. They wouldn't necessarily be standing out in the open. Still, it granted us some feeling of control about the upcoming situation. We were doing the best we could.

"If we get split up we meet at the bar, agreed?" asks Penny and we all nod.

Her hand is on the lock of the door, ready to open it and leave our lives in the hands of fate. We could all meet our end as soon as she opens it. All it would take is a hidden gunman with a clear shot. But our chances of survival might be just as slim if we stay where we are. If what Robert is saying is true, and those words weren't there when he checked upstairs, it means whoever wrote them had easy access to us all.

Maybe the only reason we're still alive is that we slept in shifts. It would have been straightforward to kill us all had we passed out at the same time. If they'd been smart about it, then we wouldn't have even heard it coming. A silencer and five swift shots to heads and our story would have ended without any of us realising we were even reaching the crescendo.

I can't remember whose idea it had been to split into shifts, but I would be eternally grateful to them for the suggestion. I'm pretty sure it saved our lives.

Penny swings the door open and we all instinctively take a step back, waiting for a bullet to whizz past us through the open door. Thankfully, nothing comes our way. No bullets, no footsteps, no sign of any human activity.

"Should we split up?" whispers Stephen, too afraid to speak at a normal volume.

"Absolutely not. Safety in numbers," replies Penny, placing her hand on his arm as a show of comfort. Tightly, she smiles at us all.

"I guess it's now or never, isn't it?" says Fiona, giving my hand a quick squeeze without meeting my eyes. Between this and the way she'd dived on top of me when the shot rang out, I was pretty certain I was on the path to forgiveness for bringing the camera.

"Everybody make your way to the pool. When we get there, try to get into the water as quickly as possible," explains Robert, reiterating the plan we've been reciting to each other all night.

"Stay as low down in the water as you can manage. It will help keep us hidden." continues Penny.

"Slow and steady wins the race." finishes Stephen, nodding his head to himself, a way to dispel his nerves I imagine.

"Let's go." I say, surprising myself by being the first to step towards the door.

Being surrounded by such powerful people is rubbing off on me. If they can pull themselves together so spectacularly, then so can I, I can step up and play my part in saving our lives. This is going to be a team effort and despite those we've already lost, I know that the five of us will leave this island on a boat together. Ready to find justice for those who have been killed. In my mind I can picture the five of us, standing in court, giving testimony. I can see it so clearly that it must be real. Bonded and maybe even friends for life.

After just two minutes of walking with a hunched back and bent knees, I can feel my body willing itself to straighten. Have you ever tried to move around in that position for a prolonged amount of time? Agony. But we have no choice. This is the way it has to be. The smaller we are, the less likely we are to be spotted.

Penny is at the front of our line, leading the way. Pausing before every corner to peer round it. Behind her is Stephen, then Robert, then Fiona, and finally me. I'm watching them all move in unison when it dawns on me.

We're moving in the order our names had been written on the wall. I want to jump to the front of the line, to jumble everyone up and misplace them. To do something to stop this temptation of fate, but I don't. To do so would only draw attention to us, and I'm not going to be the one responsible for our cover being blown.

I watch as Penny considers the jetty by the restaurant. If we used it to enter the pool we'd start out halfway across. It would be a lot easier. But the walk both to and up it would leave us completely out in the open. Which is what we're trying to avoid by using the very edge of the pool.

She turns around to look at Stephen, nodding her head towards the jetty and shrugging her shoulders. A way to ask his opinion without risking words. He considers it for a moment and then firmly shakes his head. The benefits don't outweigh the risk. And so we move in one large line towards the edge of the pool, the side closest to the complex's walls.

Robert steps forward and sits on the edge. As the tallest, it makes the most sense for him to go in first. To get a measure of how deep the water is. If it's too deep for us to walk across, then this plan might be destined to fail. All it would take is one wrong splash of an arm or leg to bring attention our way. Besides, even though I know I'm a strong swimmer – Dad had insisted on lessons from the age of six months – I can't say the same for my fellow travellers. For all I know one of them might not even be able to swim and we can't leave a single person behind. We're in this together.

He lowers both of his legs into the water and winces at the temperature of it. Cold. The sun hasn't quite arrived yet to caress it into tropical temperatures. Keeping both of his arms bent at his sides, he lowers himself down until his feet touch the floor. Standing straight, the water rises to just below his armpits; perfect.

He holds out his arms towards Penny and she follows his lead, first sitting on the edge of the pool and then allowing him to help her in. There's barely a wave as she enters the water and I begin to think that this might work.

One by one we all work together, those already in the pool helping those who are still on the side to keep any noise to a minimum. Once we're all in, Stephen nods at us each in turn, and we lower ourselves until just our heads are above water. Walking in rhythm with each other, we begin our journey across the water, the bar on the other side coming into sharper focus with each step.

Then, suddenly, I stop moving. I've had an idea. To the left of me is the wall of the complex and just below that I can feel where the movement of water is strongest. This must be where the seawater comes into the pool.

Perhaps if we can follow the tunnel out, then we can escape without having to make it to Guest Services. I mean sure, we wouldn't have our phones or Robert's gun but we would have our freedom. And it would be much easier to hide out in the surrounding landscape of the island. Besides, the killer would assume we were still within the complex, which might even buy us enough time for the speedboats to arrive. For the police to get here. It has to be worth a shot.

Checking my surroundings before doing so, I hiss quietly at the others to get their attention and thankfully they stop. Though they look a mixture of annoyed and terrified at having done so.

"There's a tunnel," I whisper, gesturing to the space by my feet. "It must go under the wall to the ocean." The hope is so strong in my body, but the cynic in me knows Stephen is about to bring it crashing down as he slowly starts walking again, shaking his head.

"Bars. It has bars on it." He explains, turning his head round to make sure I've caught his words. For a moment I want to sink to the bottom of the pool as despair tries to take hold of me. This is too hard, too dangerous. We'll never make it.

You'll never make it, whispers the voice in my head, the one that's always there to tell you that you're not quite enough. That you'll fail so you shouldn't try. The voice that's born from childhood failures and struggles, that leapt from your subconscious the first time you couldn't do something. We all have that voice, and it always pipes up at the most important moments in life.

I can't let that voice win though.

Not today.

And so I force my feet to move, crushing the fear and despair underneath my soles until it can no longer be heard. Every step leaves it further behind me as I move towards the other side of the pool, towards the bar and towards hope.

We are going to escape.

I am going to survive.

This will not be the end of my story.

I can't give up.

I won't.

Chapter Twenty

We're just over halfway to the other side of the pool now and I can see the bar.

The bar where I sat just yesterday morning, with Robert and Fiona drinking vodka and orange juice. I keep my focus on that memory as I push my feet forward under the water, painfully aware of every ripple my movement causes. All it would take was one wrong move, one large splash and the person hunting us would be aware that we'd left the villa. For now, we were operating under the belief that they still thought we were hunkered down within its walls. We had to believe that because it made us all feel safer, and made us believe that we had time to put our plan into action undetected.

Our desperate need to stay quiet is only heightened by the lack of noise in the complex around us. There's no idle chatter or clanging in the restaurant as the staff prepare for breakfast. Soon that will change. Once the sun has fully risen, people will begin their daily tasks, but for now, everyone is still asleep. Or dead. No. I mustn't think like that.

It's why the sound of a tree branch cracking underfoot somewhere is so deafening to us all. Penny freezes in place whilst the rest of us pick up our movements, determined now to get to the relative safety of the bar quicker than ever. I'm the last one to move past Penny. The others have continued on their journey with no thought for her. I guess right now it's a dog-eat-dog world, everyone for themselves and all those other platitudes that exclude you from thinking about others.

I wasn't raised to be like that though. My parents always told me that they only ever wanted three things from life for me: for me to be happy, kind, and always try my best. At this moment I could at least try to achieve two of those aims. Pausing my dash through the water, I place a hand on Penny's waist, gently I rub her back.

"It's going to be okay," I reassure her, knowing that our situation at the moment was about as far from okay as possible. But she had to keep moving.

I'd promised myself that we were all going to make it home safely and I wasn't about to leave her behind. "Here." I take her hand and give it a squeeze. Finally, her gaze moves from the bushes and plants at the shore behind us and she looks me in the eyes. "I'll go with you." She nods. One singular beautiful nod and together we make our way across the rest of the pool.

"Thank you," Penny whispers to me as we both pull ourselves up from the depths of the pool.

Fiona is the only one who waited for us. Up ahead I can see Stephen and Robert ducking from view inside the bar. Probably under the pretence of checking its safety before the rest of us got there. I was mildly irritated by their behaviour. How willing they'd been to leave Penny behind. Would they have done the same if it had been me who'd been frozen in fear? Perhaps I couldn't trust this group of strangers to keep me safe. Maybe it was naïve to think that we'd all look out for each other. Not everyone was raised to keep kindness in their hearts. Besides, as everyone knows and Robert admitted, you don't get to be top of your game without stepping on a few heads on your way up.

That didn't explain Stephen though, I thought better of him. That he was one of the people like me, someone who understood what a little kindness meant. He did work in the service industry after all.

Back when I was younger and had worked in a hotel myself, I knew first-hand how much a little kindness from somebody could brighten up a long shift. On days when I would be shouted at by guests, and even in some cases have luggage thrown at me, it was the people who stopped to show me kindness that I remembered. That I always strived to be like.

So why didn't Stephen feel the same way? If you're at the bottom of the world, as service workers are often treated, then you have to help those around you. Lift them up when you're able. Maybe no one had ever done that for Stephen so he didn't understand. If that were the case then I was determined to show kindness to him from now on.

We walk towards the bar on the gravel to lessen the spread of wet footsteps on the pavement marking our journey from the pool to the bar. I guess we hadn't fully thought the ramifications of our travel choice through.

All five of us were soaked to the bone and as we knelt behind the bar's mahogany safety, a large puddle began to drip down, formed of water from our clothing. Robert, noticing the situation, handed out cloth bar mats pulled from a drawer to each of us. We patted ourselves down as much as we were able, and one by one, removed our shoes. At least we could dry our feet if not our whole outfits.

Absent-mindedly, I pat the seal on Penny's

waterproof carry case. It's still intact and with a glance I can see that my notebook, camera and everyone's passports are still tucked away, nice and dry. Thank God for perfectly prepared Penny.

"Right, we can crawl through those bushes there to reach Guest Services," points Stephen. I could see the room of the desk just above where he was pointing. We were so close to success. Once we got to Guest Services, we could finally call for help.

"What about my gun?" asks Robert.

"I don't think that's necessary," replies Stephen.

"That isn't your decision to make." Once again, the two men were close to butting heads.

"Let's take a vote, shall we? And quickly please," says Fiona. "All those in favour of heading straight to Guest Services?" She asks and waits patiently for hands to be raised. Stephen puts his hand up and just as it looks like Penny and Fiona might follow suit, we hear a gunshot from the other side of the island and a man's scream.

Instinctively, the five of us cower down towards the ground, trying to be as invisible as possible. At least with the door to the bar closed, we could only be spotted if someone were searching for us, which at least for now, they weren't. I hoped the rest of the staff on the island would be safe. That Sam and the young man had only been targeted because of their proximity to us. It looks like I'd been wrong and that everyone was fair game.

"My staff," gasped Stephen. As though suddenly aware of the ten or so other people residing in the complex. "I have to warn them."

Forgetting about his own safety, and that of those around them, he rummages through the cupboard under the bar until he pulls out a radio. His hand is on the power button when Robert grabs his arm.

"I can't let you do that."

"You have to! They have to hide." Stephen pleads with him but Robert isn't moved by his words. "Please. Please." Stephen directs his second plea to the remaining three of us.

He's staring so deeply into my eyes I worry he's taking a measure of my soul. As much as I want to agree that he should be able to alert innocent people, doing so would mean we were swiftly discovered and killed ourselves. I try to rationalise it to myself. This isn't like when Penny froze in the pool. Helping her did not put the rest of us at risk. And even if he did radio them, who's to say they wouldn't still be hunted and killed? Who's to say they would be able to escape the island any better than we can?

No. The radio isn't the answer.

I look away from Stephen, unable to hold his gaze. Guilt over my decision is already eating me up. I thought I was a better person than this. Surely I was raised to be a better person than this? All thoughts of kindness disappear from my head and I feel a great weight of disappointment grow in my stomach. I'm just as bad as the rest of them. Willing to step over innocent corpses to ensure my own safety.

Slowly Robert pulls the radio from Stephens's hands, turns it around in his own and removes the batteries. Stephen puts up no resistance. He's deflated by our lack of action and support.

"Now, who thinks we need my gun?" asks Robert and one by one we all nod, even Stephen manages a small movement of his head.

"Wait, you shouldn't go alone." Penny seems surprised by her own concern for Robert's safety. I guess now that our escape is so near, she's beginning to remember that she doesn't like the man, not really. But her sentiment of worry was genuine. He looks taken back as well, and grateful, I think.

"She's right. No one should go anywhere alone from here on out," adds Stephen.

"Because we're all suspects, you mean?" asks Fiona, clearly still bitter about the insinuation back in Penny's villa. I don't blame her. There's no way she'd hurt Sam.

"Look. I didn't mean it that way when I said... it was a heat-of-the-moment comment that got misconstrued," explains Penny. "I know you didn't kill Sam."

"What about when you accused Robert? Did you mean that?" Fiona turns to look at Stephen with this question. Robert stands by mute as she lashes out at those around her. "Because I wouldn't blame you if you did!" The last part of her outburst shocked us all, most of all Robert, who looks as though he'd been slapped.

"You can't be serious!" he exclaims, his voice rising in volume before I reminded him to keep it low. "You can't honestly be serious right now Fi?" he asks.

"Where were you when Lucas died Robert? What about Michael? Oh yes, you were with Sam when he died. But now she's dead too."

"You're being ridiculous."

"Am I? You need to think about these answers Robert. Because the police will ask all the same questions that I am."

"If I were the killer, surely I would have just taken care of you all in the villa."

"Unless you were worried we'd overpower you. Four against one."

Silence replaces tension between them. Robert's jaw is tight, as is Fiona's. I don't know why things have just exploded between them but I wish I hadn't witnessed it.

"How do I know that you aren't placing suspicion on me to cover your own tracks?" he asks.

"Who knows? I might be. All I know is I'm better prepared for their questions than you are." It's almost as though she's accused him to show how much she cares. Almost. But not quite.

She reaches out across the distance between them and squeezes his shoulder.

"You need to be ready Robert. We all do. Once we get off this island, everyone and their dog will have a theory about what's happened here. We have to be ready for the scrutiny. We have to make sure we're always with each other so nobody can question that we are the victims."

I have to say, this side of Fiona isn't attractive to me. It's too manipulative, too forward-planning, and too selfish for me to enjoy. But I guess this is the side of her that her board members rely on.

Robert takes a deep breath, calming himself down and then places his hand upon Fiona's. He gives it a gentle squeeze.

"I know you're just looking out for me, Fi."

"Always," she replies and I've never been more baffled by a friendship. If one of my friends, not that I had many, accused me of murder, I certainly wouldn't forgive them within seconds. Perhaps he's more familiar with this version of Fiona and therefore sees the truth behind the cutthroat behaviour.

"Okay. Emma, Stephen, are you coming?" he asks and I nod like a good little soldier. I can't say I'm excited about being out in the open but I know I'll feel infinitely better when Robert has a gun in his possession. Even despite the fact that firearms give me a truly British sense of dread.

"I could come instead?" offers Fiona. Robert doesn't answer her at first. Too busy scouting out the surrounding paths, making sure we're clear to move towards his villa.

"I would never ask that of you, Fiona. What if you had to overpower me?"

He keeps his tone light but there's certainly a flash of anger in his eyes. Perhaps his forgiveness of her accusations is just skin deep. I wouldn't blame him for holding a grudge.

As much as I could see Fiona's point about being prepared for suspicion and questions upon our escape, I couldn't help but think there was a kinder way for her to make her point. A softer way. Mum always used to say you caught more flies with honey than shit, and in this particular example, I had to agree with her.

Stephen hasn't said anything in a while, not really since Robert took the radio from him. He's sat emotionlessly watching the back and forth between Fiona and Robert. I wonder if he's stuck behind the glass wall of shock. Just as I'm about to reach out to him, to try to connect and bring him back into focus, he stares at me.

"You shouldn't be here," he hisses at me as he shuffles past me, following Robert out into the open.

Fiona and Penny have heard his words and look at me quizzically. I shrug my shoulders as though I have no idea what he means. As though the stress we're under is causing him to lash out meaninglessly.

But he's right. I shouldn't be here. And I wish I had never come.

Chapter Twenty-One

It feels as though every step toward Roberts's villa is accompanied by a gunshot. So much so that after about five or six of them I no longer jump at the sound. They almost become white noise.

Stephen's face is growing darker with each one, though he makes no mention of it. It's clear it's killing him, losing his team like this, he's prevented from giving them a fighting chance. I'm a guilty party in that decision, I could have insisted that Robert let him radio the staff members. I could have thought of the other innocent lives on the island at that moment, but I didn't. I only considered the lives of those I was with. Please don't judge me too harshly for that, I should have been better, I know. I could have done more to save them, I know. My parents will be so disappointed.

Robert picked up on Stephen's sadness and, kindly, is taking the time to walk alongside him. The two of them are speaking in hushed tones, I guess to protect Stephen's privacy. But whatever Robert said to him seems to have worked as Stephen's demeanour seems ever so slightly lighter than it had back in the bar.

We come to a stop outside a villa. The door is open and the windows are smashed. I'm regretting our choice to be barefoot as we pick our way across the glass to make our way inside. A tiny shard embeds itself in the arch of my left foot and I wince in pain. Leaning against the first piece of furniture I come across, an overturned armchair, I stand on one leg and pull it out. There's no blood. Just a scratch, nothing more.

I'm just about to lose my balance when Robert cradles my arm, making sure I don't fall.

"You okay?" he asks, looking down at my foot.

"Yeah, I caught it in time." I reply, thankful for his compassion.

"Christ," exclaims Stephen as he takes in the state of the room around us.

Furniture has been flung from each corner of the room, mugs smashed against walls, paintings torn apart - somebody with a rage problem has been here. I gulp, worrying that maybe we've made the wrong choice coming here. What if whoever caused this chaos is lurking upstairs, working their way through each room methodically? We've bitten off more than we can chew. I'm about to tell Robert as much when he speaks.

"Shit." He mutters to himself looking at the damage as he picks his way through the carnage. "They can't have found it." He says to himself as he moves into the kitchen. I watch as he opens the cabinet underneath the sink and pushes his entire arm into the top of it - the man's lost the plot. We need to leave.

There's a sound of ripping and he pulls a gun from inside the cupboard. He'd taped it underneath the sink.

"Nice hiding place, Castro," I say, trying out the familiarity Fiona shares with him. I feel false as the name leaves my lips, I haven't earnt this level of kinship with him yet. He smiles at me nonetheless. He's noticed what I called him and he doesn't seem mad about it. That's a good sign. Perhaps there is hope of a genuine friendship with him once this is all said and done.

"The number one rule of gun ownership is to always make sure your weapon is safe." He's doing some form of checks on the gun before reaching under the cabinet again and pulling out what I guess is a box of bullets. Who the hell comes this prepared for trouble on holiday?

"I don't think any of that was declared on check-in," says Stephen, who even now takes his professional obligations seriously. A look flashes between the two of them, and once again, I worry that we're on the verge of a fistfight. The last thing we need is to start tearing each other to pieces. The truce they'd experienced on the walk to the villa, the emotional words that had bound them seemed to have eroded rather quickly. Still, I guess stress can do that. And maybe there will always be a part of Stephen angry at Robert and the rest of us for the murders of his team.

"We should get back to the bar," I suggest and thankfully their testosterone levels agree with me.

There's less gunfire as we make our way back to the bar, maybe they're running out of victims. Which means we're running out of distractions. God, I hate the fact that thought just crossed my mind. Please forgive me, Mum.

Fiona and Penny look relieved to see us approaching the bar. My back is killing from all the bending over but it's better than a bullet to the head.

"Everything okay?" asks Fiona.

"Someone trashed the place," Robert replies, his American accent highlighting the word trashed. I don't know why I'm fixated on that but it's comforting. I spent my life watching American shows and movies and something about their phrases and accents makes me feel at home, which is a welcome feeling given the nightmare I'm living. If I close my eyes and just listen to his accent, paying no attention to the words, I can pretend I'm at home. At the cinema with one of my friends, watching the latest blockbuster and eating popcorn. It's so easy to pretend that I don't really want to stop.

"Did you get it?" asks Penny and Robert nods, pulling the handle of the gun out of his pocket to show her. Penny grimaces, she hates the idea of guns nearly as much as me. She's very publicly campaigned for better gun control laws in the States, a stance that I'm sure her management team warned her against taking. When she spoke about the many tragedies that could have been avoided had gun control been in place, it was truly moving, so it's good to know that at least it wasn't a farce. Although, given her changing personality, I wouldn't have been that surprised to find out she was a gun-toting maniac in private.

Just as we're about to stand and pick our way across towards the check-in desk there's the sound of footsteps on gravel. Everyone freezes and I try to shrink myself down as small as possible, hoping that whoever it is doesn't decide to peek over the bar.

Stephen's face is white with fear and Fiona's jaw is quivering. Penny has her eyes squeezed shut as though that will keep the monsters at bay, and Roberts's fingers are on the handle of his gun. We're a perfect tableau of terror.

The footsteps get louder. Whoever is out there is walking down the path right next to the bar. I'm fully aware of the fact I'm holding my breath, I know that any sound we make could mean death. We listen as the footsteps draw nearer and then pause. I'm fighting the urge to peek over the bar, if I'm about to die I at least want to see the face of my executioner. That would be foolish though, I'm far safer lying here on the ground in a puddle of seawater.

The relief around me is almost physical as the footsteps change direction and move away; walking back up the gravel path and returning towards the restaurant. Whoever it was had obviously not found what they were looking for, which was probably us. I swallow a lump of nerves at the thought. We sit in the bar for what feels like twenty minutes until we're sure we're alone again. I let out the breath I knew I was holding.

"That was too close." Penny states the obvious as she finally opens her eyes, Fiona stops shivering and the colour returns to Stephen's face somewhat. Robert is the only one who hasn't relaxed yet, his hand still ready to pull out his weapon.

"Are we sure this is the best plan?" asks Stephen. "We could stay here?"

"How long until they start checking the complex a little more thoroughly?" counters Fiona.

"We have to call for help. We can't survive another twenty-four hours here," adds Penny, and she isn't wrong. The sun is rising higher in the sky now, which probably means it's near lunchtime.

We have a whole day ahead of us before the speedboats arrive to collect us, and that's if they don't slaughter the unsuspecting captains as they dock. I shudder. No. Fiona and Penny are right, we have to make it to the check-in desk, call for help, get our phones if we can, and make it out to the jetty. It's our only chance at escape.

"Why do you think they killed Lucas first?" asks Robert, his eyes out of focus. It's a strange thing for him to be thinking about right now.

"Who knows Robert? Why does it matter?" Fiona hisses at him, she doesn't have time for this flight of fancy.

"Maybe he was just the easiest one to target?" I suggest, not wanting Robert to feel bad for simply being curious. My kinship with him felt stronger since the trip to his villa. The thoughtfulness of his behaviour had grown on me.

Even I'd wondered the same since Michael had died. Before then I'd been sure that what had happened to Lucas had been personal, because of the investigations he was undertaking. Now I can't say that I believe that anymore.

"He got on the wrong side of someone," mutters Penny, peeking her head above the bar to check the coast is clear. It's an odd thing for her to suggest. If the person hunting us is simply a killer on the loose, as their crimes suggest, why would she assume Lucas had wound them up? It was much more logical to see that it was simply a case of being easy pickings.

"I don't see how this matters," says Stephen.

"I'm just trying to understand the mindset of whoever is behind this," answers Robert. And it makes sense. An unknown enemy is more dangerous than a known one. A known one you can at least try to predict. I'm not sure why everybody else is so against this train of thought – it's logical. If we can work out how the person hunting us ticks then surely we'll have a better chance at predicting their future actions and therefore surviving them.

"It doesn't matter. We've lost a criminal and a groomer, we're better off without them." Penny's words are ice-cold and she doesn't bother to look apologetic.

She means every word. Everyone turns to look at her, some in disgust at her sentiment and some, shockingly, in agreement. I'm pretty sure I'm just staring at her with my mouth agape. "He really thought he could redeem himself, thinking he was some kind of journalistic vigilante." She adds this last bit to herself, but it's loud enough for me to hear.

I bite my tongue, swallowing a world of insults about her lack of humanity. In the same way, Robert and Stephen had to keep their cool despite the tension between them, I had to follow suit. I could lash out at her in my article about this weekend when I was safely home. I'd make sure everyone knew how cold she really was. I had no worries about the ramifications for her career when she had so little regard for others.

Robert nods at us all, giving up on trying to make his point. He's decided the coast is clear and slowly opens the door to the bar. One by one we creep out from our safety net and pick our way towards the path leading to the check-in desk. Thankfully there's a line of trees and bushes providing shelter both from the sun and from anyone looking for us.

I stick close to Fiona, following her footsteps and movements as I do so. Part of me hates myself for noticing the way the muscles in her thighs swell with each step. I'd been so close to her just hours ago, and now, well now, the situation was mildly confusing. Back in my villa, she'd been furious with me, but when the shots were fired at Penny's place she'd been the one to push me to the floor. To make sure I was safe. And since then there's been little touches here and there, a brush of my arm to comfort me or a brief squeeze of my hand. Maybe, in all this madness, she has forgiven me.

We're halfway to the check-in desk now and my senses are alert, listening for any sign of danger. But everything around us is silent. No more screams or gunshots are punctuating the air, no footsteps on the path. I almost miss the sound of danger because at least then we could work out its proximity to us. The silence and stillness make me uneasy. What are they planning now? Where are they?

Penny pauses and the line follows suit. She pops her head around the tree in front of her, checking that the coast is clear. We all wait for her signal before we move again. With each step, I know we're closer to safety and I have to remind myself to not move faster than everybody else. I had to resist the urge to run for the desk, to reach behind it, and pick up the landline. I'd scream down the phone to the emergency services, demanding that they come and save us. We'd make our way to the jetty and finally, finally, we'd be free and safe.

Watching Penny lead the way it dawns on me.

How did Penny know about Michael taking bribes for the care home?

How did she know about Lucas's exposé on the matter?

I'm sure he wouldn't have confided in her about it, especially given the fact I found her name in his villa.

No. Penny Atwell shouldn't know any of those

things.
    And yet, she does.

Chapter Twenty-Two

"What's wrong?" asks Robert as he walks to the side of me. "You look like you could kill someone."

His choice of words is distasteful, and I'm sure the look I shoot at him tells him as much because he quickly apologises.

"I'm just fed up," I lie. I'm not ready to explain my suspicions about Penny to anyone, besides by doing so, I'd have to share that I went into Lucas's villa after he'd died. That might put the suspicion onto me. One thing this weekend has taught me about myself is that when it really comes down to it, I'm just as gifted a liar as everyone else. My parents would be shocked.

Penny could argue that I'm only sharing my worries about her to take the spotlight off of myself. No. It was more sensible to keep my thoughts to myself whilst keeping one eye on her. Besides, I couldn't tell Robert what was on my mind when she was only feet away from me. At first, I'd thought it was a terrorist group hunting us down. That made the most sense, especially in the political climate we were living through.

The global recession had caused people to behave desperately, it had caused there to be a lot of resentment to those who had money and success. And resentment often breeds hate. So yes. It had made perfect sense for it to be a terrorist group murdering everyone on the island. Or it had made sense until Penny had revealed information she couldn't possibly know. Now I'm certain she's behind this. I just need to wait for her to make a mistake I could cling to. One that couldn't be denied or talked around. And at least now I knew who the enemy was. I could be careful. I could prevent her from striking again.

Up ahead of us, I can now see Guest Services. Unfortunately, we'd all forgotten one thing in all the madness - the large open seating area between the shelter of the bushes and the phone at the desk. Penny's stopped moving now and we all follow suit, kneeling down in a group so we can all speak freely to each other.

"What are we going to do?" whispers Fiona, glancing around.

"We haven't heard any noises from them for a while. Maybe they're taking a break," suggests Stephen. Just at that moment, as though he'd summoned it, there was a large thud and crackle in the distance. A plume of smoke appears across the pool near Penny's villa. The pyre - they're lighting off the pyre. I remember seeing it out of the window at Penny's. I'd tried to forget the image and the fear it had induced in me.

A smell wafts its way towards us on the breeze; it's nauseating and yet sweet. I've never smelt anything like it. It's so rich I can almost taste it. It settles into my nose hairs and I just know that I'll never really get it out. Our conversation has paused as each of us takes in the scent coming towards us, everyone trying to get a handle on what it is.

"Oh god," says Robert. "Oh, no. Oh, no."

"What?" I ask, as he runs his hands through his hair, grabbing hold of it as he does so and giving it a light pull. Anxiety has very quickly gotten a hold of Robert and I wasn't sure why.

"I worked with a guy once. A stunt man. He'd been at an accident on site a few years ago. There'd been a stunt involving fire, a big explosion, a real-life one, not one of those CGI ones." Tears are coming to his eyes now as he tries not to sink too deeply into the past. "We were talking about it one day. One of his colleagues died in the explosion. Someone hadn't flipped the right switch or something. He described to me the smell. That's the thing he kept talking about, how you never forget the smell." He's rambling now.

"The smell of what?" asks Stephen, but I already know where this story is going and I heave before Robert replies.

"The smell of burning flesh."

"Shit," says Fiona. "Shit." She repeats for extra measure. Nobody speaks for a moment, as we all consider the weight of Roberts's words. The pyre - they're burning the victims on the pyre. They're destroying the evidence, desecrating their bodies, robbing their families of the chance to bury them with respect.

"What are we going to do?" asks Robert, hoping for someone to take the lead. For somebody to make the decision we all know is our only one.

"We run." I reply and everyone turns to look at me as though I'm mad. It's the only answer though. We're out of all other options. "Hopefully they're too busy, over there," I gesture towards the location of the fire, "to bother looking for us over here."

"Every man for themselves?" asks Stephen as he stares across the seating area towards Guest Services.

"Not quite. But we all just have to run as fast as we can. The first one to make it over there needs to grab the phone and dial any number you can."

"This isn't what I signed up for when I took this job," Stephen sighs and I feel sorry for him. I keep forgetting that whilst this isn't the weekend I had in mind, this is his place of work, and it's his colleague's bodies burning on that fire. I place my hand on his shoulder and am about to say something comforting when Fiona interrupts.

"Isn't exactly what we signed up for either." Rather than having empathy in this moment, Fiona is choosing to be selfish. I guess you do know the true measure of a woman when her back is against the wall. Then again, when faced with the option of saving myself or warning innocent people, I'd chosen selfishly too. I'm not so different from everyone else around me.

"I'll be contacting my lawyers as soon as I get home," adds Penny. I didn't think it were possible to like her any less than I already did. Who exactly is she hoping to sue for this? It's nobody but the murderer's fault and she won't get any money out of them.

She wouldn't be the only one contacting lawyers when we're all safely back in our homes though. I intend to make sure that my article is airtight on every level, so the public see's what she's really like. Not only has she been cold-hearted, but she knows things she couldn't possibly know. Unless she's the one behind them. It's possible she killed Lucas and Michael. She has no alibi for either.

For all I know, she's working with somebody else on the island, someone she let in through a window after putting Sam to bed. Someone who was on the roof and took a shot at the young chef. Penny's name will be mud by the time I'm through with her.

"No time like the present I guess?" asks Fiona, smiling at me as she does so. "I'm warning you though, I'm a pretty fast runner." She's trying to lighten the mood; bring a bit of competition into our situation. It isn't working. I'm still uneasy around her since seeing the 'business' side of her, the one that accused and needled Robert under the guise of caring about him. She's not quite the woman I'd thought she was.

"You're on Appleton," says Robert, winking at her. Their friendship is becoming more odd by the second, but maybe that's the way childhood friendships grow. They leave little space for an outsider to understand them.

As though someone has shot a starter pistol, Robert and Fiona sprint towards the seating area. With a shake of her head at their childish behaviour, Penny makes pursuit, closing the distance between them with ease. I can't say the same for me and Stephen. It's not like we have personal trainers at home.

I watch as Penny outstrips Robert and then Fiona, reaching the check-in desk without breaking a sweat. Robert and Fiona slow their pace, aware when they'd been beaten and instead focus their attention on the surrounding area, making sure we haven't missed any danger heading our way. Myself and Stephen soon catch up to them, and the four of us lightly jog towards Penny, who has the landline phone in her hand. There's a relieved smile on her face and then I realise what her plan has been all along. She's going to destroy the phone. Take away our only chance at safety.

I feel the air move as the bullet rips past my shoulder and the noise is sickening. Fiona grabs me and pulls me behind a nearby wall. Robert and Stephen duck for cover opposite us. We look on in horror as for one brief moment Penny remains standing at the desk, phone in hand, a look of relief on her face. She was making the call that would save us. This was all nearly over.

Then, as though she's a puppet on a string being packed away, she folds in on herself. Crumpling into a pile that we can no longer see. Fiona covers my mouth as I go to scream Penny's name.

All my suspicions and dislike for the woman are gone in a flash. I try to fight against Fiona's grip but it's too tight. I can feel her fingernails pressing against my cheek. She wraps her other arm around my chest, a way to prevent me from moving. Although I know she's only trying to protect me, it feels like overkill. You don't show someone you care by hurting them, even in a small way. I guess she's still mad about the camera.

The camera.

My hands move down to my hip where the plastic bag Penny had given me is. As far as I can tell just by touch, my camera is still in one piece, despite the way I was pushed behind the wall. Fiona must have felt me relaxing ever so slightly as she releases her grip on me.

"We have to check if she's okay," I whisper to her and she shushes me. She glances over to where

Robert and Stephen are crouched. They're on the other side of the path, behind a tall wall just as we are. I'm pretty sure you couldn't see us if you were standing at the guest desk but that doesn't mean somebody isn't going to walk down here and find us. We need to get Penny and find a better cover.

Just as I'm about to explain that to Fiona, we hear footsteps approaching. Despite her protests, I peek round the wall as much as I am able to and watch in horror as somebody walks towards the desk where Penny was standing previously. Maybe she's managed to crawl out. She could be hiding somewhere nearby. Please. Please let that be the case.

I can't make out any details of the person walking. There's a mask over their face and their stature is non-descript. I'm pretty sure it's a man but I wouldn't place a bet on it.

They have a large rifle slung over one shoulder, which they push to one side as they peer over the desk. My heart's in my throat as they approach the door Penny was running through just moments ago. The first thing they do is pull the cord for the landline out of the wall, and punch the socket. I can hear the sound as though I'm in there with them. It's the sound of my hope falling away. There goes our chance at freedom. The second thing they do is bend down, out of my view line.

By now Robert has followed my lead and is also peering around the corner of his wall. We shoot each other a look of concern. What's the gunman planning to do now?

We don't have to wait long for an answer as he emerges, bent in two, from the service door. A hand under each of Penny's armpits as he drags her from the desk. I desperately look for any sign of life from her, but she's limp. From this distance, I can't tell if she's breathing, and there's blood pouring from somewhere near her left shoulder.

"Is she dead?" Robert mouths at me as we watch the man very gently pulls Penny across the floor, away from us, and towards the fire. I shrug my shoulders.

He can tell as much as I can from this distance. If she's alive, then she's unconscious enough that she can't fight back against her captor, but there doesn't seem to be enough blood for it to have been a fatal shot. But what do I know? My medical knowledge extends to episodes of *Grey's Anatomy* and although my parents joke that I'm the family doctor - I'm most certainly not an expert.

We watch in silence until the man and Penny disappear from view.

"What do we do now?" I ask Fiona.

"We wait."

"But what about Penny?"

"It's too late for Penny."

I want to tell her that she's wrong. That she's being selfish. But I can't. Because she isn't. Once again, we have to choose between our own lives and someone else's, and once again I make the choice I never thought I would. I nod my head in agreement.

"Where do we go?"

"We need to get out of the complex. But they're looking for us now. They know we passed through here."

"So we run?"

"No. We stay here and we wait for the sun to set. We'll be safer in the dark."

Judging by the height of the sun, it's just gone midday. She can't possibly mean we wait here for eight hours before we move. That's madness. What's stopping the man, because yes, I'm assuming it's a man given their strength, coming back once he's dealt with Penny? The pavement is boiling beneath my bare feet. We need shade and shelter.

"They won't expect us to still be in this area. They'll assume the shot would have made us panic and run. That's what we can't do, Emma. We can't panic. We need to be in control of this." Her words, the sureness of them, are a comfort. So much so that I nearly forget the strength at which she gripped me just minutes ago. But my cheek still tingles from the scratch her nails left behind. Fiona is not somebody to cross, she's somebody I need to keep on my side.

"Okay. We wait." I agree.

Chapter Twenty-Three

My throat is dry and my mouth feels fuzzy.

I haven't had anything to eat or drink since we left Penny's villa this morning and it's beginning to affect me. My stomach growls in protest at its emptiness and Fiona shoots a look at me as though it's something I can control.

She had been right about waiting here though. We have seen no one since Penny got shot. They must be busy on the other side of the island, searching for us in every nook and cranny. Getting more and more frustrated as they fail in their hunt. I knew it was right to trust in her instincts and I was smart enough not to question them.

Stephen and Robert have stayed on their side of the wall and I've been intensely jealous of them. On their side, there is a generous amount of shade from a nearby tree and I've watched as they've taken it in turns to sit in it. All we have for shelter is a, frankly, very prickly bush which Fiona has generously let me sit in on several occasions. It's no use though, my skin has been badly burnt by the sun. I can feel the ache of it already forming, which is a welcome distraction from the pangs of thirst and hunger. I'm fighting sleep every minute we stay hidden here, a sign of heat stroke and dehydration, I'm sure. If we have to run, I'm not sure I'll have the strength to do so.

The sun is beginning to set now, and I've never been more grateful to see the back of it. If I thought the heatwaves in England were tough, they were nothing compared to this. At least, even when stuck in my sweltering and humid flat, I had access to cool running water and ice pops to keep myself sane. I can't think about water right now. About the dripping faucet in my kitchen. My lacklustre water pressure in the shower. The cold, sweet taste of water readily available to me.

Fiona places a hand on my arm.

"Are you okay?" she asks. Her voice sounds croaky. She must be feeling just as dehydrated as I am.

"I need a drink." I rasp at her, aware that in the grand scheme of things, dehydration wasn't the most dangerous thing we were facing, but it was the one at the forefront of my mind. She considers my request and then nods.

With a quick sprint, she moves over to the boy's side of the wall. I can't hear their conversation but whatever she suggests, they both readily agree. I watch on in exhaustion as Fiona and Stephen leave the safety of our cover and pick their way toward the Guest Services desk. I'm too weak to call out to them, to tell them to stop whatever they're doing, but I can't. I'm delirious with thirst, and right now, I'd consider taking a bullet for a drink.

Robert catches my eye across the short distance between us and gives me a thumbs-up. It's awkward. Unnatural. But still, I smile gratefully at him. I watch as Fiona and Stephen disappear through the door and reappear behind the desk. Their heads held together tightly as they exchange words. She says something to upset him. I can tell, even from this distance, by the way he shakes his head and steps away from her. She smiles at him, a detached smile I've not seen on her face before, and leans in closer to his face as she whispers something to him.

Whatever it was seems to have worked as Stephen returns her smile. All is well between them and I watch happily as they quickly walk back towards us, arms full of water bottles and snack packets.

"We're always prepared for our guests checking in after the kitchen has closed," explains Stephen as he returns to Roberts's side of the wall. Fiona drops her stash at my feet with a proud look on her face. She's happy she's been able to help me. I can't help my greed as I lunge at a bottle of water, bring it to my lips and chug half of it back in one go.

"Thank you," I gasp as I finally convince my body to remove it from my mouth. She's made no move towards the water or food yet and I glance down at it. "Aren't you going to?" I ask, nodding down at the collection at my feet.

"You go first. I fast regularly so I'm okay for now."

She doesn't have to offer twice as I pick up a small pack of biscuits and rip them open with my teeth. The Emma before all of this would have worried about how that might look to others, but I don't. The Emma before would have wanted to eat daintily and with a sense of self-control in front of a person she was attracted to. The Emma before was a fool, I think to myself as I shove a shortbread into my mouth in one go. Its buttery comfort explodes on my tongue and I gasp in ecstasy.

This amuses Fiona and she picks up a packet of nuts, opens them, and then offers them to me. This is the Fiona I fell for. The kind, thoughtful woman I'd read so much about. I didn't need to worry about the other side of her I'd seen earlier, or about the way she'd left scratches on my skin when she'd had her hand over my mouth. That was all just the drama of the situation we were in. That wasn't the real her. I knew the real her. She'd given me the real her this weekend.

"What happened with Stephen?" I ask between mouthfuls. Her face changes in an instant. The sweet smile she'd been watching me with fades.

"What do you mean?"

"It looked like you had an argument when you were getting the supplies."

"The man is an idiot," she answers, the smile returning to her face as she leans in closer to whisper to me. "He was actually concerned that we were stealing supplies from the hotel. Can you believe it!"

No. I couldn't believe it. Nobody is that much of a jobsworth.

"Anyway," she continued, leaning back away from me now, "we'll be making a move soon. Best get your strength up."

I do as asked and continue stuffing my face with the snacks around me and drink two more bottles of water. We still have at least sixteen hours by my count until the speedboats are due to arrive, and I'm not sure when I'll get the chance to eat and drink again.

Fiona drinks half a bottle of water and eats a handful of nuts. Maybe when we get out of this, I'll try fasting as well, and ask her for some pointers. It would be nice to be as strong-willed as her. And it never hurts to take an interest in other people's interests, does it?

Robert and Stephen make their way across the open space between the two walls to join us, and as we all finish the last of the food and drink, I feel like I'm attending some kind of twisted picnic.

"So, I guess now we try to get out?" asks Robert as he leans back on his hands. I can't help but feel we've all grown a little too relaxed in this moment. Like we've all forgotten the danger that's lurking around us. We've been safe and alone for too many hours now. We're starting to believe it's over. But it won't be over until I'm safely back in England with my family. Only then will I relax.

"Shall we take a picture?" asks Fiona. I'm startled by the question. It's the first time she's mentioned my camera since she found it beneath my pillow and this is hardly the time to take a selfie. I'm about to tell her it's a terrible idea when Robert laughs. The noise is too loud and I want to tell him to stop, instead a giggle floats up out of me. Soon we're all hysterically chuckling and I'm holding the camera out in front of me, ready to take a photo.

Once we've all got our sanity about us, we start planning our escape. The doors aren't very far from us. We could easily make it if we ran. Once out of the complex, we'll find cover near the jetty so we can warn the captains of the speedboats what's happening and make a quick getaway. Or we can personally greet the police. Whichever happens first we'll be ready.

Robert and Stephen are scouting the area around us when Fiona grabs hold of my arm. She gently squeezes it.

"If anything happens, I want you to keep that photo. I want you to remember the good parts of this weekend." She's talking about the before. The games on the flight over, the laughter over our first (and last) meal together, and the kiss we shared before everything turned into a horror movie. She wanted me to take that photo for me, so I would take something good away from this experience.

"Nothing's going to happen. We're going to be okay." I reassure her and she smiles at me, tears pooling in the corner of her eyes.

"I really wanted more from this weekend."

"Me too." And then she leans forward and plants a gentle kiss on my lips. It feels like a goodbye. Like she's seen my future and knows she isn't part of it.

"We stay together." I say to her, taking her by the hand. "We stay together and we survive together." She nods at me and wipes her eyes. I hope my words have given her faith because all I want right now is to survive. For all of us to survive.

Robert appears at my side. "We're ready to go if you are." he sighs heavily. I look at Fiona. The nerves have faded from her eyes and she looks back at me fiercely, squeezing my hand to let me know she believes in my words. I will make sure we survive.

"We're ready," she answers firmly, not letting go of my hand. But I'm not ready, not yet.

"I have a question," I say and Robert and Fiona turn to look at me. The three amigos reunited. "Did anyone else find it strange what Penny said back at the bar? About Lucas and Michael?"

"I'm sure she didn't mean to sound quite so blunt," assures Robert. I'm glad that he too noted the lack of empathy from Penny at that moment. Although I'll never share the friendship he has with Fiona, I hope that when we get home he at least keeps in touch. The three of us together like this just makes sense to me. It feels right. Hopefully, Robert Castro will stay my friend when this is all over. I'd like that. As for Fiona? Who knows. Maybe we'll pick up where we left off in my room.

"It's not that. How did she know those things?" I have to keep my mind on the task at hand, escaping the island. If I focus too much on the 'what comes after' then I might miss the chance to run.

"What do you mean?" asks Fiona, still holding my hand.

"How did she know about Lucas writing an exposé? Or about Michaels's crimes?" They're both staring at me blankly and I remember that I've never clued them in to all that I know. "I only know those things because Lucas told me on the first night. Out on the jetty. So how did Penny know?"

They both consider my question, and I'm relieved they aren't instantly throwing accusations my way. Then, Robert's face clouds over.

"I saw something in Penny's room when I checked the windows. I didn't think anything of it at the time but now you've pointed it out," he closes his eyes, trying to drudge up the memory. "There was a notebook on her bedside table. With the initials LJ on it."

I'm floored. Penny had Lucas's notebook. That's how she'd known. But why would she have it unless she'd snuck into his villa to steal it? And if that was the case, why did she act so shocked when Stephen announced his death? Lucas's villa was one of the few here that had a lock. There's no way she could have broken in to take it. She had to have gone in after he'd died. After Fiona had broken the garden door. But why?

"You aren't thinking…?" asks Fiona as though she can read my mind. "But she's dead. She can't have anything to do with this."

"Unless she's not. Dead, that is. I only saw a wound to her shoulder. What about you?" Asks Robert, looking at me. Only the two of us had watched her body be dragged from behind the desk. I shake my head.

"No. I didn't see any other wounds."

"She's dead. She's definitely dead," says Fiona, and I wish I could agree with her but now there was doubt. If I couldn't trust what I'd seen with my own eyes, then I was in serious trouble.

"We need to leave," I say with certainty. If Penny really is alive, if she's somehow involved in this, then she's simply been toying with us. Leaving us alone for this long when she knows where we are. Waiting for us to relax and let our guard down. She knows that we have Robert's gun, that we aren't completely defenceless. We can't stay here any longer. She could change her mind and come for us whenever she wants.

The three of us move across to Stephen, who's waiting on the other side of the prickly bushes that had offered me some level of shade.

"So we just run?" he asks, unsurely.

"We run and we stick together. Make it to the jetty," I say, not sure when I'd become the decision-maker in our group. A role that, until recently, had been Penny's.

The four of us nod at each other and take a deep breath. Robert takes my hand in his, just as he had on the plane all those hours ago, and shakes it. His grip is warm and firm.

"Look after my girl?" he asks, nodding at Fiona. She blushes under his attention and I nod my head.

"Always," I reply. He smiles at me, he believes me, and he knows I won't let anything happen to her.

Then, without a countdown, we start running to the open entrance doors. Fiona's hand is tight in mine as we move in sync.

The world around us explodes in gunfire and the doorway is so close now. My thighs ache with excursion and my palm is sweaty in Fiona's. The gunfire grows more rapid and it isn't until I'm sheltering in the woodland outside the complex that I realise my hand is now empty.

Chapter Twenty-Four

I'm sorry if the pages are wet.

I'm trying to write about everything that's happened since the last time I had a minute and it's all caught up with me. I don't think I'm crying but the wetness on my face and my running nose tell me otherwise. I shouldn't be sitting here terrified and crying, I should be doing something heroic. Something to save the day. But it all seems so futile.

I don't know what happened to the others.

I've been sat here for an hour now, waiting to hear any sign of them but there's nothing. I'm all alone. I'm not even sure that the others made it out of the complex if they're still alive. Everything just happened so quickly. I never meant to let go of Fiona's hand. Or did she let go of mine? I just can't remember. I can't picture it. I don't want to. If I let go of her hand then it means I lied to her. I didn't keep her safe. It means I broke my promise to Robert to look after his friend. It means I betrayed them both. And if she let go of my hand then that means…

I can't think about what that could mean. Not right now.

No matter how much it upsets me, I have to write everything that's happened down whilst it's still fresh in my mind. Whilst I can still smell the burning flesh, and hear the crackle of the fire waiting for me, so I don't forget anything. This will all be important information when help arrives.

It will help the police know exactly what happened and when. I don't know if I'll be able to tell the story again after this, not in this much detail. As soon as I've written it all down, I hope it slips away from my memory, like a nightmare just after you wake. I don't mind being left with the fear, I just don't want to be left with the memories.

I want to forget everything that has happened since we found Lucas's body and go back to my normal life. If it meant I could go back to being the Emma before I'd even consider giving up the memories of the good moments too. The time I spent with Fiona and Robert. How the three of us bonded. I'd give it all up if it meant I could just be me again.

I'd give anything for a normal Sunday night right now - to be sitting in my PJs, mindlessly scrolling through Rebecca's countless emails, preparing myself for the work week ahead. An episode of *Schitt's Creek* on my small TV as I stuff my face with a takeaway pizza. I'd call Mum around six pm, to check in and see how her weekend's been and then I'd take myself off to bed to lie awake for hours worrying about my to-do list. I just want to be normal again.

Mum, Dad - if I don't make it home, then I want you to know how much I love you. I really do. The two of you are the reason I am who I am and I'm so sorry if what you've read makes you think you failed as parents because you haven't. You were phenomenal parents. I just made the wrong choices along the way this weekend. I should have fought for Stephen to be able to radio his team. They were just as innocent as we are and they deserved just as much chance to escape. If their families read this, please know, from the bottom of my heart, how much I regret that decision.

Dad - your impressions of Robert were actually spot on. It's amazing how well you learnt to mimic his laugh. I know I used to tell you it made me cringe or get stroppy and storm off when you did it, but I know you were just teasing me. Finding a way to connect with me, to make me smile. I'd have never admitted it to you at the time but it did make me laugh. Truly it did.

Mum - I really hope you get to meet Fiona. You'd really like her. You've always supported me, in everything I've ever done, never once making me feel you didn't love me unconditionally. I know how lucky I am to have that. Some of my friends' parents certainly didn't give that to them. I'm so grateful for every single thing you've ever done for me.

Rebecca - your passwords are in an Excel sheet on my desktop. If you don't know how to open it, ask Linda.

Wait.

What was that?

I swear I just heard somebody shout.

No. It must have been my imagination.

I'm getting too caught up in writing out these notes of what could happen to me in the next few hours before salvation arrives. I've just got to stay hidden and then this self-indulgent page of my notebook can be ripped out and forgotten.

Shit. There it is again.

A man's voice.

He's shouting out the word "why?"

God, I don't want to move. But I have to. We'll be safer together.

Stand up. Take a deep breath. Move.

Chapter Twenty-Five

I'm running towards the sound of the voice. I can hear an argument but I can't make out the words. I don't care about the loudness of my steps or my heavy panting as I move. All that matters is that I find them.

Foolish I know.

For all I know, I'm running straight into the arms of the people hunting us but all the logic in my mind has been replaced by desperation. It has to be them. It has to be.

"Why?" I hear the man shout again. It's Stephen. I'd recognise his voice anywhere, even when it's lacking its usual derision.

Just as I'm about to call out to them to let them know that I'm here, that I'm safe and nearby, a gunshot ripples through the air around me. I dive to the floor.

Birds appear everywhere in the sky, startled by the sudden intrusion on their peace. Penny has found us. Penny has found us. Penny has found us. Those four words run on repeat in my head like deathly poetry through my mind.

I have to be brave. Now is the time for action, not anxiety. Penny can not win. I will not let Penny win. I have the element of surprise on my side.

If she's with them, then she doesn't know I'm out here. She might have assumed me dead, just as I'd assumed her. It's delicious irony and I'm almost grateful for the gunshot that prevented me from revealing my position. This could be my opportunity to save us. All I need is to get the gun from Penny. Hopefully, the shock of seeing me appear will distract her and then the four of us can overpower her. The odds are in our favour.

I'd promised Fiona we would survive.

I'd promised.

Despite my protesting muscles and rising anxiety, I push myself up from the ground. Being careful now to keep my movements small and quiet, I pick my way through the foliage, towards the spot I'd heard the gunshot ring from.

I hear them before I see them. Two voices. Male and female. Both filled with fury. Robert and Fiona.

All I can hear are hateful expletives being thrown between them. There's nothing logical I can put my finger on. No clear words to warn me of what I'm about to walk in on. I pause and listen for a moment longer, trying to pick out Penny's voice amongst the argument but for now it's just them. It's safe. With a deep breath, I take a step forward, out of my hiding place and into the belly of the beast.

"Holy shit!" shouts Robert in Fiona's face. There's barely an inch of space between them. I can see spit flying from his lips and landing on her cheeks.

"Emma!" She screams as she spots me, breaking away from Robert, who reaches out a hand to stop her. She swats him away with ease. Tears are streaming down her face, her hair is knotted and full of dirt. As if she's been rolling around on the floor. Looking down at Robert's hands, I see that they too are covered in a mixture of mud and sand. Have they been fighting?

"Emma!" says Robert, also stepping towards me.

I hold my hands in the air and they both stop in their tracks. There's a tingle at the base of my spine and a feeling in my gut I can't ignore. Something isn't right.

I have to take in the scene around me. Now that they've moved, I can see something on the ground, just feet behind them.

"Is that..?" I can't finish my question because I already know the answer. Stephen is lying on the ground. A hole where the back of his head used to be. Brains, bones and blood seeping into the ground around him.

"He's gone mad Emma, you have to listen to me," pleads Fiona, reaching for one of my hands.

"Don't listen to her. She's a psycho," retorts Robert as he shoves her away from me. She falls to the floor and cowers below him. He raises a hand to strike her and on instinct I step forward placing myself between them.

"That's enough, Robert," I say. Fiona's right. He's gone mad. The terror around us has broken him mentally. I need to understand what's happened here. I need to know where Penny is hiding so we can move in the opposite direction. She must have had Stephen picked off from range, which means somebody could be out there, watching us through a scope on their gun, waiting for the orders to pull the trigger.

"She killed Stephen," says Robert. His voice is a touch calmer now he's speaking directly to me. "She shot him in the back of the head."

"You're the one who brought the gun Robert," she says, pulling herself to a stand whilst being careful to keep me safely between her and Robert. She's genuinely afraid of him

My head is spinning. Penny did this. Penny had to have done this. Maybe she drugged them the same way she did Michael, causing this paranoia? Something in the supplies we got from Guest Services, but then surely I'd be feeling the effects too?

"I don't understand," I say, because I simply don't.

"She's been behind this whole thing! Stephen was working for her and she killed him. She just killed him."

"Bullshit. Fuck you, Robert. You did this. You did all of this."

They push me away from them and begin to hit, kick and scratch at each other. If I didn't know any better, I'd say I was witnessing a fight to the death. But the two of them are friends. Childhood friends. They don't actually want to kill each other. Do they?

I cry out in pain as the fall twists my ankle but neither of them stops to pay me any attention. That's when I spy it, lying over in a mound of tall grass. The gun.

Robert's sitting on Fiona's chest now, hands around her throat. She's gasping and spluttering for air. I need to get them to stop. They have to stop fighting if I'm going to make any sense of this.

Despite the throbbing sensation in my foot, I hobble over towards the gun. It feels foreign in my hands, lighter than I'd imagined. I hold it out in front of me, finger on the trigger like I'd seen in the movies, and point it at the two of them.

"Let her go Robert," I demand. He doesn't pay attention to my words and now Fiona's thrashing is slowing. He's killing her. "I said let her go."

I squeeze the trigger, a very risky move I know, and a bullet embeds itself in a nearby tree. My shoulder muscle flings back with the recoil and there's a ringing in my ear, but it's worth the pain because he finally pays attention and loosens his grip around Fiona's throat.

"Now get off of her."

"Please, Emma, you have to believe me. I'm doing this for us, to keep us safe." He follows my order but pleads with me as he does so. I watch as Fiona wheezes air back into her lungs and slowly sits up.

"Think about it," he continues, "who else here could afford to put something like this together? Who else here has that level of influence? She's always been there just after someone died, just enough time to create an alibi. It's too much of a coincidence."

"I was with Emma when Lucas was killed," protests Fiona, rubbing her neck.

"You were with Emma when Lucas was found, maybe not when he was killed."

"You're mad. Honestly. You've lost it. Where were you when Lucas was killed? What about Michael? Oh yes, you were off with Sam who's now conveniently dead." The two of them are staring daggers at each other whilst I stand mute, pointing the gun at them. Someone here is lying. But I don't know who.

Stephen couldn't have been in on it, could he? There's no way he'd sacrifice his staff members like that. I saw the look on his face when we heard the shots. He was devastated by their murders. He was desperate to radio and warn them. There's no way he did this.

But then.

Then there was the argument he had with Fiona in Guest Services. The whispered conversations between him and Robert on the way to retrieve the gun. His constant reminders that I didn't belong here. The irritation, or what at the time I'd thought was pain, in his voice when he exclaimed he didn't 'sign up for this' when he took the job on the island.

If Stephen was in on it, then it was Penny he was working for. Penny, who never had an alibi. Penny, who knew things she shouldn't. Penny, who had motivation and kept a trophy from Lucas's murder.

"No. No. Penny did this. It was Penny. We all said it was Penny." My words are all over the place I know, and my hand is shaking from holding the gun upright for so long.

"That's what she wants you to think,"

"That's what he wants you to think,"

They speak in unison, two voices, and one sentence. One lie and one truth.

Frustration crosses Roberts's features and he takes a step towards Fiona. I change the aim of my gun to point directly at his head.

"Emma," he keeps his voice calm and turns his attention back to me. "Emma, you know me. I've been by your side throughout this. Why would I put myself in danger if I was behind this?"

"Why would I?" interrupts Fiona and she has a valid point. Why would either of them put themselves through the hell of being hunted when they could have hidden away? They'd both put themselves in danger numerous times as we'd travelled from Penny's villa to the outside of the complex. Only a true psychopath would consent to that.

"Emma, Emma, please. Listen to me, please listen. What reason would I have to do this? Why would I put you in danger like that?" Her voice is soft and it pulls at my heartstrings. Time and time again Fiona has looked out for me. From pushing me to the ground when bullets were first fired, to risking her own skin to make sure I didn't collapse from dehydration. She cares about me. She really does.

Then I remember the smile on her face as she whispered something to Stephen at the check-in desk. That wide smile that didn't reach her eyes. The way she hounded Robert about his alibi, telling him she was more prepared for scrutiny than he was. Would a sane person be busy building a defence in the midst of a killing spree? I don't know.

"She doesn't believe you." Something in my face must have given my doubt away because Robert seems gleeful. "Thank God she doesn't believe you."

Then I think about the angry looks and constant bickering between Robert and Stephen. The kind an out-of-control manager might have with an underling. The secret about Lucas's moral crimes Robert shared with me. His exasperation when Fiona and I first came to him with our theory about a murderer being on the island with us. He would barely entertain the idea. Fiona was right. He didn't have an alibi for either of the first two deaths. And he could have closed an open window after Sam was killed to cover his tracks.

I switch positions, pointing the gun at Robert one second and then at Fiona as my mind tries to process and separate fact from fiction. They're like two caged animals, ready to spring at the other as soon as they have a chance.

"We're all going to stay like this until the police get here," I announce, having made a decision. The sensible decision, I believe. So long as I had them at gunpoint then I had the situation under control.

"Emma, that's twelve hours away. You won't be able to keep him here that long."

"I'm happy to stay here. So long as I have eyes on Emma, at least I know you can't kill her."

"I would never hurt Emma."

"But you'd kill everyone else, yes?"

"You're a psychopath, Robert. You need to be put down."

"They'll give you the chair when we get home. I'm going to have a front-row seat."

"Do you actually believe your own lies? The words that are coming from your mouth, do you actually believe them?"

I let them continue their accusations, back and forth, each getting more outlandish as time wears on. All I need to do is keep the gun steady and the two of them stuck to this spot. The police can work out the rest.

But my arm is already so tired, my muscles are not used to holding the same position for so long. Not to mention the gruelling weekend my body has been subjected to, both mentally and physically. I'm suddenly so tired. Twelve hours is a long time. Fiona's telling the truth about that at least.

"Why was Stephen shot in the back of the head?"

My attention keeps being drawn to his corpse, a morbid curiosity. I've never seen a gunshot wound this close. I didn't realise we had so many brains inside our skulls.

"He'd had enough of her plan. She offered him

more money and he refused."

"No. We were all talking. Stephen needed to take a leak and Robert shot him point blank."

They both sound like horrifically plausible explanations. I don't want either of them to be true, but one of them is, the evidence of its truth is laying on the floor just in front of me.

Something pops up in my memory, waving its arm around frantically to try to gain my attention. The word I'd heard the man shout - why? He'd asked. Neither Robert nor Fiona's stories matched what I had heard with my own ears. That question wouldn't make sense in the context of either of their stories.

"Why?" I ask, hoping to jog their memories. Instead, they both go to tell me the same story, I interrupt them. "No. Stephen asked why?"

For a moment they're both stunned into silence. They'd been unaware that I'd been close enough to hear his shout. Robert recovers the quickest.

"He wanted to know why she would break their deal."

Fiona scoffs at his words and looks at me, her eyes wide and pleading. She's begging me to believe her.

"It's because I told Robert I would help him get away if he let us live. Stephen wanted to know why I still valued his life after everything he'd done."

We stand in silence for a moment before Robert bursts out laughing. It's not the same laugh he's had before, not the one I've heard in countless interviews. This laugh is unhinged, full of desperation.

"You should have been an actress." He chokes out the words between bouts of delirious laughter. "Please Emma, tell me you aren't falling for this? Why would she try to save Stephen after everything we've been through? You saw the way she spoke to me back there. She as much as admitted to being the killer but we didn't pick up on it!"

He isn't wrong. When I cast my mind back to that argument between them, the one in the bar before we went to retrieve Roberts's gun, she had seemed like a different person. And what was it she'd said when he'd pointed out that she could be the killer? 'Who knows? I might be,' was what she'd said. At the time it hadn't seemed so out of place. She was being flippant, I'd told myself. Looking at those words now, they hold a different weight.

If whoever was behind this had been in our group the whole time, they must have gotten a sick pleasure out of every moment of fear we felt. Drinking it in as they played along. Knowing they were behind it. And why wouldn't someone like that also enjoy the fact that they more than admitted to being the guilty party and got away with it?

I move the barrel of the gun an inch until it's pointing at Fiona's chest. She gasps in shock and I have to fight the guilt I feel at the terror in her eyes.

"Emma, no." is all she can say. "No. No. Please."

"I'm not going to shoot you Fiona. I'm not going to shoot anyone. We're all going to wait here until the authorities come."

"You can't last that long alone, Emma. You'll need to rest. Let me help you." Robert's voice is soft, relaxed, he's finally feeling comfortable that I've made my decision.

"I don't need your help," I say, wiggling the gun in his direction to ensure he knows that he's still a suspect. "As long as you both stay exactly where you are, everything will be okay."

"You sound like the bad guy," whispers Fiona, refusing to meet my eye. She's not wrong. As much as I'm bringing a murderer to justice, I'm also holding an innocent person hostage. Better to hold them hostage, though, than have them become another victim, I rationalise to myself.

"I'm not going to hurt you. I promise." It turns out that even when faced with the possibility that my holiday fling might be a cold-blooded killer, I still want her to like me. That takes people pleasing to a whole new level.

My eyes keep flitting between the two of them, as though a sign will suddenly appear, flashing and neon above one of their heads, reading the word 'liar' in fluorescent lighting. It doesn't, though. This decision is solely mine.

They're both right. I might have the upper hand now but that could change in an hour or two. Twelve hours is a long time to stay standing in one spot holding a gun. A long time to keep your attention focused laser-sharp on two people. I haven't slept since the night at Penny's villa, which was nearly twenty-four hours ago. The water and snacks we squirrelled away in the complex won't be enough to keep my belly full until help arrives. I can't do it on my own.

An idea strikes me.

"I'm going to tie you both up." As ideas go, it's a pretty solid one. If I tie them both to a tree, away from each other, then I can at least guarantee neither of them can escape. Then I only have to worry about staying awake. I'll be able to sit down at least.

"With what?" asks Robert, looking around us. He's willing to go along with my plan, but has rightfully pointed out the flaw in it. Contrary to my wildest hopes and dreams, a yard of rope hasn't magically appeared at my feet to allow me to bind them. Fiona hasn't spoken since she pointed out I was behaving like the bad guy. Instead, her eyes have been firmly fixed on her own feet. She's dejected, given up all hope of freedom. Or escape. Whatever way you look at it.

As I'm about to try to engage her in conversation, to grill her more on the situation, there's a massive explosion from inside the complex.

Flames and smoke billow high up into the sky. The noise makes me physically jump so rapidly that my hands lose their grip on the gun.

Now I no longer have the upper hand, fear returns to my blood. One of these people is a murderer. And I don't know who.

I run as fast as I can.

Chapter Twenty-Six

This can't be happening.

This isn't happening.

This isn't real.

I stood on some kind of thorn as I was running away from Fiona and Robert. I couldn't stop to pull it out until I was safely away from them. It's in there really deep, now. I need to remove it but I can barely hold my pen right now and I don't have anything I can use to grip the protruding end with.

It doesn't matter though. The thorn. What's a thorn in the foot compared to a bullet in the head?

I'm hiding back in the same spot I was before I heard Stephen shout. Before I walked into the most confusing situation of my life. There's a lot of shade here and I think that will help keep me safe.

I think there's about twelve hours now until lunchtime. It's pitch black out here. I'm using what little moonlight I dare to write this. All I have to do is stay hidden for twelve more hours and I'll be okay.

I heard a gunshot as I was running away.

Just the one.

There was no scream, no one shouting in pain. I don't know if it was one of them or the gunman from the complex. Either way, I'm staying as still as possible. They will not find me. I will not die here. I won't die here. There's no way Fiona or Robert will kill me. Their argument in the clearing was all based on a misunderstanding. Paranoia brewed up by Penny and her underlings. Neither of them are behind this.

They can't be. They wouldn't.

Something crept over my leg about two minutes ago and I nearly shrieked because even without being able to see it, I knew it was a spider. I hate spiders. But I remembered I had to be quiet at the last minute and put all the terror into my cheek and bit down on that instead. It bloody hurt.

I've tried to make myself as small as possible since I hid.

I'm lying on my side, legs tucked in towards my chest and head propped up with one hand. It's not the most comfortable position but it will do for now. So long as it keeps me alive, anything will do for now.

****

It's been two hours since I heard the gunshot. Or that's what I think anyway. I've been checking the time on my camera sporadically, aware the light from the screen will highlight my hiding place. I looked at it when I first got here and just now.

The actual time on it is wrong of course, it's so ancient it doesn't update itself automatically when the clocks go forward or back, plus the time difference between here and home is, gosh, I can't remember the time difference. I should be able to remember the time difference, shouldn't I? But either way, two hours have passed between the time it showed me when I hid and now. That's good. It means I only have ten hours left until help gets here. I can do that. It's just ten hours.

That's five movies. Twenty episodes - a series basically. And I've definitely sat and binge-watched a series in a day without noticing the passing of time.

This will be like that.

It will be lunchtime soon and I'll be home before I know it.

****

Somehow I fell asleep.

Not for long, but long enough to leave me feeling a little more alert. I think it's somewhere between late at night and early morning now; the time of day you usually only see if you've been out-out and had a good night. It's been years since I've had a proper tear-up. I'm definitely going to have one when I get home. Maybe I'll see if some of the girls from the office fancy trying one of those 'bottomless brunches' that are all the rage right now. After this weekend I think I could drink the bar dry.

The battery on my camera is flat so I don't know how long I've been out here. I can make out the horizon from where I'm lying and it seems hazy. Maybe the sun's going to rise soon. That's good in a way as it means I'm closer to escaping, but bad because I think I'm going to have to find somewhere new to hide.

I realised whilst sitting here that there are actually a lot of bald spots in the bushel I'm hiding in. Spots the sun will easily highlight. All it would take is the wrong person walking past at the wrong moment, and I'm worried that there are only wrong people left on this island.

So I'm going to have to make a run for it. Over by the jetty, about two hundred yards away, I can see a bunch of rocks and trees.

They're near the ocean as well, so at least I'd have access to some form of water - I know sea water isn't the ideal thing to drink but honestly, something has got to be better than nothing.

I need to move now before the sun rises and although I haven't seen anyone or heard anything since that gunshot, I know they're out there still. I can feel their eyes searching for me - annoyed at me for escaping.

My left foot is throbbing now. It's red and angry where the thorn still is. I've picked at it as best I can, but my nails just aren't sharp enough to pull it out. My right ankle is twisted from where I fell after the explosion, but I don't have a choice. I have to suck it up and make a run for it. Wish me luck.

****

I made it.

I might be hyperventilating, but I made it.

I'm closer to the complex walls now and the smell from the pyre is sickening. Whoever is behind this must still be in there because the fire seems to be burning as heavily as it always has, they've got to be feeding it constantly to maintain that level of heat.

I wonder if Robert or Fiona's body was on there now. I wonder if they've saved a space for mine.

That's not going to happen, though. I won't let that happen. The sun is rising but I feel confident my spot is more secluded here. The seawater tastes salty and I want to spit it back out, but I do manage to force myself to drink two handfuls. That will help. I need to keep my strength up and my wits about me. I'm not going down without a fight.

I keep thinking about my parents.

Of how they'd spur me on. They've always been my cheerleaders, and it helps to think of their support in this moment. I don't think so much about what they'd suggest. They don't exactly watch survival movies or anything like that, but I like to think of them standing by my side, reassuring me that all my decisions are the right one - that they are the ones that will bring me home.

I'm going to rest for a while, collect my thoughts and catch my breath - the run over here really took it out of me.

****

I think it must be morning now. As in proper morning. The sun has fully risen, but isn't yet at its peak. Hopefully, I've only got a few hours to go.

A little while ago I heard footsteps approach my hiding spot. No voices. No rustling as they searched the foliage for me. Just footsteps as though someone was just taking their daily walk. All I wanted to do was peek over the rocks I'm hiding behind and see who it was. But I didn't, because they might have seen me. And because I might have seen them.

I might have seen Robert standing there, covered in the blood of his childhood friend, false Hollywood grin as he offered me his hand to lead me to salvation.

Or it might have been Fiona out for a walk. Stretching her legs after murdering everybody on the island, steely glint and twisted smile on her face.

I didn't want to see either version of those people, and so I stayed hidden until the footsteps disappeared. Mum says that was the right choice.

****

The sun's at its halfway point but I haven't seen anyone yet. My eyes have been staring out at the ocean almost permanently since I noticed we were approaching lunchtime. The speedboats should be here now. That's what Stephen had said, wasn't it? That we were going to go home on Monday lunchtime?

Maybe that had been a lie, too. Maybe the people who picked us up from the airport had been in on this as well. What about the pilot of the plane? Did he know he was delivering us to our death?

No. I have to stop this paranoia. It won't do me any good.

A while ago, I found a sharp stone and used it to dig the thorn out from my foot. It had been a mistake.

I'd nearly screamed out in pain a couple of times but I'd held it together. Now my foot is a bloody mess with flaps of skin and open flesh. I should have just left it well enough alone, despite the throbbing driving me mad. Dad stood next to me as I dug it out, cursing my stupidity and impatience.

I hadn't considered having to walk across the sand barefoot with an open wound. That is going to be sore.

Mum gave me a long talking to once I'd calmed down, told me all about infection risks. And she's right. I could have put up with the throbbing for another couple of hours.

No. She didn't say that. She's not here. Neither's dad. I'm alone. Safely alone.

When help arrives, they're bound to have a first aid kit. They could have taken the thorn out carefully and with minimal damage. It was an impulsive decision but it was done now. I couldn't do anything to change that.

What I could change though, was my grip on reality. I had to remember that no matter how much I wanted them to be, my parents weren't here with me. They can't talk to me. They can't lecture me and they can't scold me. My imagination is running away with itself.

It's late afternoon now and still nobody has arrived. Where are the speedboats? Where are the police?

Fuck.

Shit.

Bollocks.

They never called the police, did they?

I'm so bloody stupid.

I've been holding onto the fact that the police are trying to reach us when, really, Stephen never called them. Because why would he if he was in on the plan? We just took his word for it. We never saw him place the call after all.

What if this means no one's coming?

No.

We're definitely booked on a return flight home. I saw the ticket myself. Even if the speedboat men are in on it when we all fail to board, an investigation will be launched.

They will come here straight away. There's no way they won't given the stature of the guests I'd travelled with. Their agents, lawyers, and families would be on the phone, chartering private jets and boats to get to the island to find out what's delayed us.

Any minute now the cavalry will arrive. I just have to be patient.

It's early evening now. I'm not going to lie, I've felt quite a lot of despair these last few hours. It's why I haven't written. I didn't want to share it. Didn't want to tell you how scared or alone I feel. Because I'm going to survive this. I am going to survive this.

The footsteps came back about twenty minutes ago. They paused just on the other side of the rocks that shelter me, almost as if they were teasing me with their proximity. And if they know I'm here, then I have to move.

I have a plan, though. One that Stephen gave me. When we'd been crossing the pool and I'd spotted the tunnel that led to the ocean, he'd told me it had bars across it.

The sea is receding at the moment, which means I could swim out to the other end of that tunnel and hide within it. They'd never think to look for me there.

And I'm sure help will arrive before the tide comes in. And when I see or hear anyone arriving, I'll be sure to get their attention before they dock. Maybe I'll even be able to swim out to meet them.

I'm not risking anyone else setting foot on this island of horrors. If they step foot on the jetty, then they might never step off. I won't have another soul dying this weekend. Not one.

I'm going to bury my notebook and the bag though. I don't trust that it will be waterproof enough for the amount of time I need to be in the ocean. It's fine though because once I'm safe I'll come back for it and everyone will know the truth of what happened here. Even if I haven't quite figured it out myself.

I will be there, in court, when they sentence whoever was behind this. I will look them in the eyes and they will know that they did not break me. Because they have not and will not. I am going to survive. I am going to go home, back to my normal life, and survive.

I am going to quit my job, though. You can take this as my notice, Rebecca. Life's too short not to chase your dreams and I need to do more with my time than book you trains and take the blame for your mistakes.

So, for now, this is the last of my notes about this weekend.

I hope I can still make sense of them when some time has passed. I'm going to carefully pull out a few stones and hide the pack within the pile, that way the sun won't bleach them if it takes me a while to get back.

Which I imagine it will. When the police arrive they'll want to cordon the whole island off for evidence, and by God, they'll have their work cut out. Hopefully, I'll be able to convince them to retrieve this stuff for me. I'll make sure they understand how helpful my notes could be in piecing together what's happened this weekend and where.

I'll write soon. I promise.

Chapter Twenty-Seven

And that's it. That's the last of Emma's notes. A promise she would never keep.

Just as she'd guessed, everything happened the moment their return flight remained grounded at the airport. Private security, the FBI, Scotland Yard - you name it, they rushed to the island.

Lucas, Michael, Penny, Robert, and Fiona were valuable commodities to people who had the right connections and no expenses were spared as private jets, speedboats, and even yachts were diverted in the race to arrive at Hotel Horizen first.

Emma's family didn't have that kind of manpower behind them, but they did get on the first commercial flight they were able to. They arrived Tuesday evening just after news of the horror had broken.

Needless to say, they were devastated to have heard the story via social media rather than being briefed by the official team investigating.

The FBI was the first to land on the island, and therefore they took the lead spot in the investigation. By the time they'd arrived though, part of the hotel itself was aflame, and with no way to put it out, they had to sit on board their boat and wait for it to die out naturally.

The pyre Emma described was being used to burn bodies as the victims had suspected. Charred remains were recovered and some were identified, others were so badly damaged that they're still working on the formal identification. Dental records have been useful in at least two cases so far.

Did you know that you can't really build a fire that's warm enough to burn human remains in its entirety? You can burn the evidence off, of course, but the bones remain, or at least the calcium phosphate remains. But it's nearly impossible to build a fire in the wild to the temperature required to burn bones. Plus, fire is temperamental. It moves as it likes and when it runs out of fuel, it runs out of heat. The fire at the hotel ebbed and flowed its way around the complex, meaning no area had stayed hot enough for the fire to burn all remnants of its victims.

To fully disguise your victims, you have to destroy the bones, drown them in acid or grind them down into pieces. That's what it turns out they'd done to a couple of the bodies, smashed the bones into shards after the flesh had been removed. It's a sign of the true depravity that had existed on the island.

Lucas, Robert, and Fiona were only identified because amongst the debris, the agents found a handful of teeth belonging to the three of them. Michael's remains were left intact and were the first to be logged in the case.

Emma and Penny have yet to be formally identified but even now, six months after that weekend, the crew is still combing the island for evidence. At least once a week a new body part is discovered. So far the official death count stands at sixteen, including staff members.

Lucas's family has officially been informed of his death thanks to the notes and photographs Emma took of his body. Her pack was discovered two weeks after the FBI began its investigation and it's been integral to their process. Stephen's body was found partially eaten in the jungle where Emma had last seen him. Along with blood splatters that have been assigned to Robert and Fiona. Nobody knows the truth of what happened in the clearing. The running theory is that Emma snapped under the pressure and her paranoia slipped onto the page. Weight was only added to this idea after Robert and Fiona were formally identified as victims. Unless this was some kind of murder-suicide, then it made no sense for them to have been behind it.

What's widely accepted as the truth is that this was the work of a small terrorist group, the 'eat the rich' killers as they've been dubbed on some online forums. Disenchanted with the global cost-of-living crisis, they took their frustrations out on a group of millionaires, torturing and murdering them to prove a point. Quite what the point was, we aren't sure and so far no group has come forward to lay claims to the crimes.

The actual contracted staff for Hotel Horizen had been stranded out at sea on that Thursday evening. Drugged and placed unconscious onto a boat, they'd spent the weekend mindlessly bobbing around on the ocean waiting for help. Thankfully, they'd been left with adequate supplies, or the death toll would be higher than it currently is. I guess even the 'eat the rich' killers have a heart - at least when it comes to the so-called common man.

When the staff were finally located, rescued, and cleared of any wrongdoing, they identified Stephen and Sam as the two who had drugged them. After viewing both their passport photos the staff members were adamant that they were behind the whole thing.

They'd pretended to be a couple on their honeymoon who had gotten swept out with the tide from the local town whilst on a romantic boating trip. The staff had welcomed them into the complex, checking them over for any signs of dehydration or heat exhaustion, and had offered them a place to stay for the night. The plan had been for Stephen and Sam to hitch a ride back in one of the speed boats after the true guests had been dropped off. That never happened, of course.

The police would have assumed that Stephen escaped had it not been for the words in Emma's notebook leading them to check the surrounding area ahead of their schedule. No doubt this annoyed the forensics team, who were painstakingly sweeping the island metre by metre looking for evidence, but at least it gave the police evidence that Emma's words were true.

Stephen had been the ring leader. That much is clear from his bank statements. He received a payment of two million dollars the week before the crimes and had distributed $50,000 into twenty separate accounts. Each of those bank accounts so far matches with a body found in the pyre. That left a cool million for Stephen alone.

Investigators believe that one of his colleagues found out about this and snapped, just as their plan was reaching its crescendo. That's who they believe is the real person who shot him in the back of the head. They then went on to hunt Fiona, Robert, and Emma before finally killing themselves for reasons unknown. The working theory is they were driven mad by guilt which to us seems implausible.

Stephen hadn't been lying about the only boat on the island being damaged, but it had been done maliciously. Parts of it were strewn all around the bank of the island, out by the maintenance shed. Fingerprints were lifted off an axe found nearby but so far they don't match any in the database. It's the same story with the guns that were found neatly lined up by the entrance to the complex. We believe this was staged, a way to make people believe that those behind these crimes simply gave up - we've not been able to prove anything as of yet.

Whoever was behind these killings had a hell of a financial backer. Aside from the transfer into Stephen's accounts, somebody supplied the killers with ammo, weapons, and a mode of transport to the island. They also paid for new identities for everyone involved to use once the slaying was complete, identities that they never had the chance to use.

Michael's family has tried their utmost to prevent the publication of these notes, as though what they contain isn't already in the public domain.

An internal investigation is going to be launched into his involvement with the care home's building companies - his current wife has yet to comment. She's holed herself up in their holiday villa in Spain, citing grief as a reason she's unable to return to England for questioning. His first wife reportedly laughed when somebody broke the news of his death to her.

Penny's wife has taken over her talk show. She spent the first episode apologising and explaining her affair with Robert. It was a moment of madness during a dark spell in their marriage, something they were working through together. I don't believe she should be discussing it all so publicly whilst there's an active investigation but her press agent pushed for her to take over the talk show, a way to ensure that Penny's legacy and charitable efforts live on. At first, audiences tuned in to see if she would give away any clues as to Penny's whereabouts, but eventually, they grew to enjoy her presenting style and the viewership figures remained steady.

Lucas's name is now mud. Somebody managed to hack into his personal social media accounts and several message threads with girls aged seventeen, on the cusp of eighteen, were found. It turns out that in each instance he first met them or connected with them online when they were fourteen. The messages, whilst innocent at first, soon take a flirtatious turn. So Robert had been right in what he'd told Emma. Lucas wasn't a paedophile but he wasn't far off.

Robert's father has given up his retirement from the spotlight to allow the blockbuster his son had been working on to be completed. He agreed to stand in for him, and with the help of some miraculous makeup, physical therapy, and CGI, he completed reshoots as his son's character. It's set to be the biggest box office opening in cinema history.

Fiona's cousin has been appointed to run Appleton's printing industry. He's always been in her shadow, waiting for his time to shine and now it's finally here. The stocks are dropping, though, as people's faith in the company's longevity waver. He's adamant they will recover, though, once the investigation is closed - and is pushing for this to happen as soon as possible..

As for Emma's family, her father has remained stationed on the mainland near the island. He hasn't left since the couple first arrived six months ago and he remains steadfast in his belief that his daughter will be found alive. He won't return to England until she's back in his arms.

Her mother returned two weeks after arriving to retain a legal team to make sure justice was served. She told us in our first meeting that's what Emma would want. Her daughter had always believed that life should be fair, that rights and wrongs should be rewarded and punished as needed. We are working for the family free of charge, as this is a sentiment we thoroughly agree with.

The sad fact is, despite her father's hope, we have no reason other than to believe that Emma passed away before help could arrive. It may not have been by the hands of the assailant, though. As she said, her plan had been to hide in the tunnel that led to the complex's pool.

Unfortunately, she would have been suffering from malnutrition, dehydration, sunburn, heatstroke, and the infected injury to her foot. The warm and calming flow of water around her most likely lulled her into a light sleep and she would have floated unconscious out into the sea. A boat goes out every day to search for her body, but so far, it has found nothing. It's unsurprising. The ocean is vast and the tide could have carried her anywhere.

Without any suspects at the moment, there is no court date. You can't punish someone for a crime when they, as far as anyone can tell, don't exist. We have faith, though, that this will change one day. The person who is truly behind all of these murders is too smart to have thrown themselves on the pyre. They planned too thoroughly for it to end in their death.

They are out there somewhere and they will be found. Everybody makes mistakes eventually.

Our working theory is that Penny truly was behind the crimes of that weekend. There's no reasonable explanation as to why she had one of Lucas' notebooks in her bedroom, plus there were no witnesses that could confirm the shot had killed her. We believe she agreed to a superficial bullet wound to throw suspicion off herself. Plus her body has yet to be identified in any way. There is no single trace of her on the island which given Emma's suspicions only proves, in our mind at least, that she had something to hide.

So now, dear reader, you know the full story. Perhaps you have your own theories, maybe you and your book club will discuss them over a glass of wine and some crackers. But when you do talk about that long weekend, we hope you keep in mind that there were real humans behind each chapter. Real lives that were lost. Try to have empathy when you speak of Emma and what she lived through.

One day we hope to add an epilogue to this book, an update on the case, and the answer to the question that might live with you nearly as long as it's lived with us - who did this?

Until then, be assured that we, and many law officials and local volunteers, are doing all we can to put the pieces together. If you have any information you believe could help the case, then please contact my office and we'll be happy to discuss it with you. There is no cash reward at the moment but this is something the families are all negotiating between themselves.

Thank you for your time.

Christopher Bailey
Attorney - Hanson, Cherry & Kearney Associates

Epilogue

"You're a best-seller babe," I say to her as I walk into her room.

She doesn't reply. She never does. It's been six months since we left the island and she's spoken about that many words to me since we escaped.

At first, I put her ignorance down to shock. I wasn't so twisted that I lacked empathy for her situation and what we'd been through together.

At times during that weekend, I'd even felt some level of terror - and I was the mastermind behind it. I always knew how it was all going to end, but that didn't stop me from being genuinely afraid once or twice. One of those times had been near the end of the ordeal, when she'd pointed the gun at me.

I was so certain she'd seen through my façade, seen the truth about the situation before her. I was ready to strike before she did, not that she noticed. She'd never handled a gun in her life, that much was clear from her stance. She at least held the gun in two hands but her foot position was all wrong. She stood with her feet planted horizontally when really, had she adopted the Weaver stance I was a fan of, she should have been distributing her weight on her forward foot. When she'd fired the warning shot, I was certain she'd pulled a muscle in her shoulder. I'd longed to step forward and correct her stance, to show her how she was doing it incorrectly, but that would have been a misjudgment. That would have given the game away.

So instead I'd been forced to bite my tongue as I watched the woman I was fascinated with making rookie errors. She was braver than I gave her credit for. Not smarter though. She still fell for my lies.

I'm sure she'd give anything to go back in time to that moment. To make a different decision. To put a bullet in my brain as I had in Stephen's. Those regrets of hers will fade though, when she realises I've given her everything she wanted. Her notebook is on the New York Times best-seller list, it has been for weeks. It was Oprah's top pick - all things I know that Emma once dreamed about, because she wrote about it in her notebook, before she started telling the story of that long weekend. The first dozen pages are full of her hopes and dreams and it's through them that I've gotten to know her on a deeper level.

Of course I read it.

I'd watched her bury it in the rocks and as soon as she was apprehended from that blasted tunnel, I'd picked it out, sat down with a glass of wine and read it front page to back. She was a talented writer, a little harsh in her character assessment at times, but I knew she created something special. A new legacy for the two of us. I wasn't a fan of some elements of her tale of our weekend together, but I left them in there because they made the story more engaging. They help humanise her to the public, and I would hate for the public to see her as 'one of us.' She deserves better than that.

She'd been right. I had been toying with her the few times I'd walked past her hiding place. I'd known where she was all along. Always had. I wasn't going to let anything bad happen to her, which is why I had her dragged, kicking and screaming, from the tunnel.

If I hadn't, she most likely would have drowned, having underestimated the speed at which the tide can turn out here. I sedated her and we sat together on the beach, waiting for my boat to arrive. It had been a wonderful moment. It would have been really romantic if she hadn't been drooling from the multiple shots it had taken to keep her still. The time for romance will come though.

When she's ready to listen, I'll explain everything to her properly. I'm not wasting my story on someone who doesn't care to hear it. I'll tell her how I was left with no choice. Because that's the truth. My family's legacy was crushing to live up to. My father's ever-present shadow was so enormous it prevented me from blossoming to my full potential. He still insists on accompanying me to every large-scale event, a way to show a united front.

No matter how hard I worked, I would never be allowed to leave the hamster wheel. I was the face of our family and everything relied on me, my successes, and my reputation. I'd be trapped in that position until the day I died, and what kind of life is that?

Over the years, to keep things running as they should, I'd made too many promises to the wrong kinds of people - people who would also never accept my retirement. No. I had no choice. This was the only way out, the only way to guarantee my freedom.

If I'd been the only one to 'die' that weekend, it would have sparked suspicion in the minds of those I'd rather not cross. It would have been too convenient a tale for them to swallow. They would have carried my scent in their hearts and hunted me like a fox. I had to think bigger than that. My plan had to be flawless, unquestionable, and tragic. And everything had been set in place, everything had been perfect. Until Emma's arrival. She's been an anomaly I hadn't planned for.

An innocent trapped in a web of the rich and lawless insects around her. I wasn't going to spill her blood just to achieve my aims. I do have morals, you know.

The others who died are of no great loss to the world. Some of them had committed actual legal crimes, others were guilty of crossing moral lines, and a few I just couldn't stand. Either way, their deaths will not keep me up at night.

What had kept me up at night, however, had been the ache in my jaw from the missing teeth the back alley dentist had pulled the week before my trip. That had hurt. It had almost felt a waste to throw them into the pyre with the bodies after all the pain they had caused me. But each time my jaw ached, I reminded myself that they were a small price to pay for a bigger picture. My freedom.

I'd relished my time on the island. Enjoying the game a little too much at times. Planting red herrings where I was able.

I'd trashed Lucas's room after he'd been killed, making sure to add Penny's name onto one of the pieces of paper scattered artfully on the floor. I'd relished the moment, really enjoying destroying his life's work after the fight he'd put up. Having seen how much he'd drunk, and slipping a few crushed sleeping pills into one of his beverages, I'd expected it to be an easy kill. But boy did that man have fight left in him. I guess that's what happens when you feel righteous about something. Thankfully at the time we found his body, nobody noticed the scratches I'd left on his arms as I'd lashed out at him, determined to wrap the noose around his neck. I almost blew my cover though when I tidied away the stool I'd used to tie him to the beam. Honestly, I don't know what possessed me to do so. It was my only mistake from that weekend, but in the end, it turned into an enjoyable one. Listening to Emma as she waxed lyrical about it being evidence of foul play was thrilling.

Killing Michael had been fun. I'd splattered red paint around his room after drugging his coffee. It only helped escalate his paranoia, he believed it was blood. Placing the drugs inside his jacket pocket had been a stroke of genius, I'd nearly congratulated myself out loud as we held him under the water. Politicians and drugs - it was such a cliche. I'd watched as the oxygen bubbles grew smaller and smaller until finally he was gone.

My favourite move though, was planting one of Lucas's notebooks in Penny's bedroom. I knew she'd read it. How could she not? I'd expected her to let the cat out of the bag sooner than she had, but still, it had been delicious to witness when she eventually cracked and let her knowledge of what Lucas had been up to slip. I had hoped somebody else would have noticed it on her bedside, but nobody useful had.

Taking Penny's body with us had been a stroke of genius inspired by Emma's notebook. She'd been so passionately sure of herself when it came to distrusting Penny that I couldn't resist. Readers seem to have gone along with her theory for the most part so I made the right decision. We sailed for two straight days before I finally threw Penny's body overboard. I watched as it sank into the ocean, never to be discovered. Emma unwittingly gave me the perfect scapegoat for my crimes.

I'd had to rely on my exterior assistant when it came to shooting the young chef and slicing Sam's throat. It was too enjoyable being amongst the victims at that time, feeding off their fear gave me a high I worry I'll be chasing for the rest of my life. A window left open gave them the perfect opportunity to climb in and do what needed to be done. I'd snuck up and written the list of names though when everyone was asleep. The team that was supposed to be keeping watch alongside me didn't have the staying power I did. It took me ten minutes to write our names and five minutes to carefully retrieve Emma's camera and take the picture. What can I say? I was quite proud of my penmanship and I wanted to escalate the terror felt by those around me.

Stephen had grown quite tiresome as the days wore on. Shooting him in the head was both about self-preservation and because I wanted him to shut up. All weekend he'd been bickering with me about the plan, changing his mind at moments he really ought not to have. He'd known all along that the rest of his team was going to be murdered and yet he still had the audacity to want to radio them and warn them after he'd explicitly agreed to this term at the beginning of our agreement.

Thankfully, he'd been stopped though. That would have been a nightmare. Besides, other than Sam, he had no real connection to any of them. Just a bunch of snowflakes he'd met in various forums that wanted their shot at 'eating the rich'. God, I hate that phrase. It's just so distasteful. Why not just say kill the rich? Surely it has the same level of poetry as that clunky motto.

So when Stephen had wanted to radio his team, he'd meant it. That's when I knew for certain that he had to go. We'd had a quick chat after that and I'd promised him a bonus when the weekend was through. That managed to calm him somewhat, at least for a while. But then, when we were in the clearing, he had to go and run his mouth. The death of Sam had been harder on him than he'd expected and he wanted me to stop. He wanted us to stop right before the finish line. That wasn't going to happen so I shot him as he stomped away.

The fight over the gun before Emma arrived had been unfortunate, but I'd misjudged my childhood friend. Hadn't been expecting their reflexes to be quite as sharp as they were. Still, it didn't matter. Emma was so conflicted between our stories that she couldn't make a decision. Then she dropped the gun and ran, leaving me with a chance to take care of business.

My only regret over that weekend was that I didn't get a chance to kill Rebecca Marsh. She'd been the one I'd been most looking forward to dealing with. Her death would have been one of the personal ones rather than one of the moral ones. The only sin she'd ever been guilty of, as far as I could tell, had been her birth. She was the product of an affair between our parents, you see. A constant reminder that my father didn't love my mother as he ought to.

I've met Rebecca countless times throughout my life, both at public and private functions, and never once has she hinted at her lineage. No thinly veiled references to our shared bloodline so I assume she doesn't know. You might argue that it's not her fault she was born, that she didn't make our parents sleep together. But it wasn't my fault that my father didn't love us enough to stay loyal to our family. She should never have existed. The universe had not planned on Rebecca Marsh's presence and I would simply have been reapplying order to the chaos her birth had caused. Yes, leaving her alive would always be my biggest regret. But I guess now that I have my freedom I can always clean up that mess another time.

Confronting my father about my half-sister had been the last conversation we'd had before his 'accident,' before he became too old to keep up the work he loved so much, the work that I stepped in to take over. He apologised relentlessly, but it had meant nothing. My mother didn't even know the truth, and I made sure to keep it that way. Not out of loyalty to him, but out of love for her. She didn't need to experience the same betrayal I had.

I've lived in my father's shadow for the last two decades. I'm done protecting his legacy, though, done continuing his 'good work'. It's time for me to live my own life on my terms, away from my family name and all it means to the world.

Emma will grow to understand all of this. I know she will. You can't fake a connection like the one we'd had on the island. The few conversations we'd shared had been genuine, I was sure of it. She was a kind soul. She'd shown me compassion and empathy. I needed that in my life.

If the slaughter had never happened, I know she'd have fallen in love with me. I know she would. I saw the care in her eyes when she lowered the gun and chose to believe me. She wanted to believe me. Because she cared about me.

"Netflix is going to adapt the book, you know?" I say.

She finally turns to look at me. Her eyes are bloodshot and there are dark bags under them. I must pick her up some sleeping pills when we next dock. She needs the rest. Her hair is weighed down with grease. It no longer frames her face perfectly, and her roots are overgrown. I wonder if any of the crew knows anything about styling. Perhaps I can learn to box-dye her hair for her. I think she'd suit a lighter brunette this time. The colour she arrived on the island with didn't suit her in my eyes. She's losing weight rapidly despite the meals that the chef prepares for her. I make sure she always eats the same meal that I do - I want her to become accustomed to the life I'm providing for her. As I've said, I'm not a monster.

The room smells of rotten food and body odour, and I hate to admit it, but these visits are getting harder for me every day.

In the beginning, when we first set sail, I couldn't get enough of her company. I'd come down here and read, not bothered by the silence or disdain emanating from her. I knew it would pass. I'd hoped it would.

Maybe I was wrong though. Maybe she isn't the girl I thought she was. I'd give her one more week before I made my final decision on the matter.

With a sigh I sit down on the armchair in her room, trying to pretend I don't hear the way her chains jangle as she makes the effort to roll over and turn her back on me. Not interested in my company or conversation.

I'll give it one last try for today and then come back in the morning. Maybe by then she'll have finally changed her attitude. I know this next sentence will get her attention. She always pays attention when I mention their name - she can't resist.

I have to admit, the pain on her face when I do so almost makes up for the jealousy I felt when she didn't choose me that first night after the meal.

I can't say I blame her. I wasn't blind to my friend's beauty, I'd just always assumed my charm would beat it. Still, every couple makes mistakes.

Granted, not everyone has to read about their partner's holiday fling in quite such graphic detail, but I'll get past it. One day, all of this will be a funny anecdote we tell our friends. A saucy aside Emma can tell the girls over brunch as they gasp at her dabble into lesbianism. Just a small paragraph in the grand stage show of our lives together.

So, when I ask her my last question for the day, although I know it will upset her, it is with hope that one day we can be more upbeat when we look back on the people we lost and left behind that weekend.

"Who do you think they'll cast as Fiona?"

ABOUT THE AUTHOR

Steph is currently working on a number of standalone psychological thriller books which will be released soon.

For updates and pre-order notifications on future publications please consider signing up to the mailing list or following SM Thomas on your platform of choice.

Acknowledgements

Thank you as always to my family and friends for their support whilst I've been lost in Emma's world, my ideas would all still be stuck inside my head without you guys cheering me on.

Thank you to my editor Allison for not reaching across the Atlantic Ocean to slap me when I disagree with a comma placement.

And thank you dear reader for taking a chance on an indie writer, please know that every time somebody purchases an indie book a fairy gets its wings. (Well, not quite but you get the gist.)

Now go forth and work your way through the rest of your TBR pile, I'll see you there!